PRICE
OF
DUTY

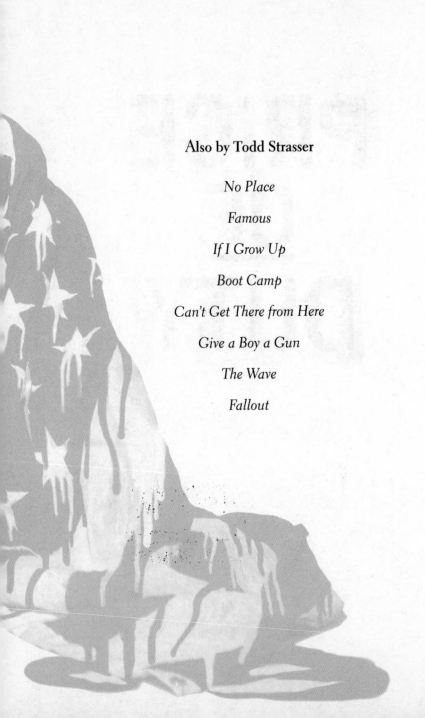

Also by Todd Strasser

PRICE OF DUTY

TODD STRASSER

SIMON & SCHUSTER BFYR

New York   London   Toronto   Sydney   New Delhi

SIMON & SCHUSTER BFYR

An imprint of Simon & Schuster Children's Publishing Division

1230 Avenue of the Americas, New York, New York 10020

SIMON & SCHUSTER BFYR is a trademark of Simon & Schuster, Inc.

For information about special discounts for bulk purchases, please contact Simon & Schuster Special Sales at 1-866-506-1949 or business@simonandschuster.com.

The Simon & Schuster Speakers Bureau can bring authors to your live event.

For more information or to book an event, contact the Simon & Schuster Speakers Bureau at 1-866-248-3049 or visit our website at www.simonspeakers.com.

Jacket design by Lucy Ruth Cummins

The text for this book was set in Electra LH Std.

Manufactured in the United States of America

First Edition

2 4 6 8 10 9 7 5 3 1

CIP data for this book is available from the Library of Congress.

ISBN 978-1-4814-9709-1

ISBN 978-1-4814-9711-4 (eBook)

To the young men and women
of the United States Armed Services.

"War does not determine who is right—
only who is left."

—BERTRAND RUSSELL

My thanks to David Gale, Petra Deistler-Kaufmann, Amanda Ramirez, and Stephen Barbara for their guidance, suggestions, support, and patience.

PRICE

OF

DUTY

ALJAHIM

You are trained to be a soldier, not a hero. But sometimes the other thing happens.

BOOM! CRAUNK! Both sounds are unbelievably, painfully loud. Loud beyond imagining. Like your head being smashed between metal garbage can lids. So loud you can't believe you'll still have eardrums afterward. If you have time to believe anything. But you don't. There's no time.

A moment ago you were riding down a road in a Humvee. Now the vehicle's lying on its roof forty feet off the road and you're the only one left inside. Heavy munitions fire, screams, shouts, and explosions join the loud ringing in your ears. Metallic *plangs* ricocheting off the Humvee. Thudding *pocks* when rounds slam into the bulletproof windows. Inside the vehicle, you're hanging upside down, restrained by your seat harness. Half a dozen burning points of pain are distributed around your body.

Vision is a reddish blur. An IED headache has your brain in a death grip. Something warm is running up your cheek and into your right eye. It's bright red.

Someone nearby is screaming, *"I'm hit! I'm hit!"* Someone farther away is shouting, "Where's the triggerman? Find the triggerman!"

Bratta! Bratta! Bratta! Plang! Pock! Zang! Multiple weapons fire. It dawns on you that there is no one triggerman. There are dozens.

Boom! The Humvee is rocked by the blast of an RPG.

"Ahhh! Ahhhh!" More screams of pain.

Where are my buddies?

My eyepro's gone. There's nothing to protect my eyes from flying shrapnel and dirt. The reddish blur in my vision is blood. It's coming from a piece of shrapnel lodged painfully under my chin cup. How it got there, I'll never know. It's one of a dozen pieces of shrapnel that the Army docs will eventually remove from my body.

But right now most of those shrapnel are just vague burning points of pain. Right now it's all adrenaline, shock, shouts, and explosions. I'm upside down. Rollover training kicks in. Orient, establish three points of contact, brace, and release the seat harness. Egress. My gloved hand jerks the door handle, but the door won't open. Wait, my head is closer to the ground than my feet are. In this position, you don't push the door handle down. You pull it up.

An instant later I roll out into the heat, sunlight, and

mayhem. Intense machine gun and small arms fire bashing my eardrums. Supersonic lead bees whizzing past. But the firefight is good news. Someone on our side must be shooting back. The hot air stinks of gasoline and sulfur. A fusillade of bullets rips into the ground, spraying grains of dirt into my face and mixing with the blood in my eyes. I'm in the kill zone, in what must be far ambush conditions. How do I know it's not near ambush? Simple. If it was a near ambush, I'd be worm dirt by now.

More metallic bees whiz by. The closest ones cutting through the air inches from my head. I get prone, jam some QuikClot under my chin cup. Damn, that hurts, but it stops the bleeding. Blink the remaining blood out of my eyes and try to establish where the enemy fire is coming from. Glance around for cover. Where are my guys? Skitballs, Magnet, Clay? Remind myself that I'm in a mined area. I can't stay exposed like this for long without getting hit. But where will the land mines be if I move?

These thoughts race through my head in a matter of milliseconds.

"*Ahhhh! Ahhhh! I'm hit! Jake! I'm hit!*" It's Skitballs. He's somewhere to my right, where a lot of enemy fire is coming from.

I have to go get him.

JAKE

The prop plane touches down. I can see the crowd through the window. They're cheering, waving American flags—some small, some large. A handwritten bedsheet banner reads: WELCOME HOME, JAKE! OUR HERO!

A homemade cardboard sign taped to a broomstick: THANK YOU FOR SERVING OUR COUNTRY.

There must be two hundred people out there.

My heart beats harder. I've had weeks to prepare for this moment. Weeks to rehearse what to say and when to say it. Yes, I'm supposed to be a hero. I've been told that a thousand times since the ambush. Only I don't feel like a hero. When it's actually happening, you don't know you're being brave. You just do what you've been trained to do. What your instincts tell you to do.

You do it knowing there's a good chance you're going to die. You do it because you have to . . . if you hope to be able to live with yourself when it's over.

The plane that's brought me home to Franklin is provided by a company that collects donated miles and uses them to fly war heroes and wounded warriors around for "nonmilitary purposes." As we taxi toward the terminal, I start to recognize faces—Dad, Lori, Aurora, and the General are out in front. I've seen them dozens of times on Skype over the past six months, but now, seeing them this close makes my heart ache. I've missed them. It's going to be so good to be home.

The crowd can see me through the plane's window. They're waving, pumping their signs up and down, shouting words I can't hear through the glass. Meanwhile, my heart is drumming, my body taut at condition orange. My hands don't want to obey when I try to undo my seat belt. It's safe inside this plane. I'm protected . . . and alone.

Come on, Jake, I tell myself. *No one out there wants to hurt you.*

This should be easy, right? Just go out there and see your family, your friends, and a couple hundred adoring neighbors. Instead, it's as stressful as being in the lead Humvee of a convoy. As much as I've been looking forward to seeing everyone, I've been dreading this moment for weeks.

"Jake?" The pilot's come out of the cockpit and is leaning on the seat in front of me. He has a ruddy face and a mustache. Gray sideburns poke out from beneath his pilot's hat. With that frozen smile people wear when they're trying to mask concern, he nods at the window. "They're waiting for you."

"Yessir." I unbuckle the seat belt. Ironically, at moments like this, it's military training that gets me to do that which I wasn't sure I'd be able to do. My left leg juts out into the aisle because it's in a cast from the top of my thigh to my foot. I grab a crutch with one hand, and the top of the seat in front of me with the other.

"Need help?" the pilot offers.

"No, sir. Thank you, sir." I hoist myself up and position the crutches. Duck my head down the narrow aisle and turn out through the doorway. The crowd cheers, raises their banners, and waves flags. There's everything short of a brass band. The sun is bright and I'm glad I'm wearing shades. It feels hot for early June. With the scent of honeysuckle in the air come memories of carefree days lounging by swimming pools, flirting with pretty girls.

If only I didn't know now what I didn't know then.

I start down the airstairs. At Landstuhl, they taught me how to do stairs with crutches and not fall on my face. The plane's props have stopped turning and the cheering crowd surges forward. My body goes tense, on alert. You can tell yourself that these are family and friends, that this is secure and sheltered America, not a war-plagued foreign land filled with snipers and suicide bombers. But you can't simply turn off training and experience. My eyes dart automatically, searching for the telltale metallic glint of a weapon, the unnatural bulge of a suicide vest under a shirt.

Halfway down the steps, my heart is racing. My body

may have returned home, but my brain is still wired for war.

My family waits at the bottom of the airstairs. Lori and Aurora have tears in their eyes. They slide their arms inside the crutches, hug and kiss me. I'm enveloped in the different scents of their perfumes. My heart swells. It feels safe to be with them. They try not to stare at the jagged scar on my chin. They've seen it before on Skype, but here it is for real.

Dad pulls me close. "It's great to have you home." He seems to be blinking back tears.

The General gives me a bone-crushing handshake and claps a hand on my shoulder. "Congratulations, son. We're proud of you. You're a tremendous credit to our family."

Aurora keeps her arm around my waist and nestles close. The fragrance of her light brown hair delights my nostrils. I'm so glad to see her, so filled with gratitude that she waited for me. Plenty of guys had girlfriends who didn't. But she wrote letters and sent candy and thumb drives with movies on them. And she was almost always there when I wanted to Skype. What I've been through was bad, but it would have been so much worse without her.

This is the last stop on the "hero tour." My right wrist is sore from all the hands I've had to shake. I've learned to keep my left hand low at my side and in a loose fist. That way the damage is less noticeable. But my sister, Lori, knows what happened and reaches for it.

"Not here," I whisper.

The rest of the crowd presses in. My body stiffens. I've been on anti-anxiety meds for weeks. Otherwise, I might be doing a combat roll right now. But even with the pills, I'm still wound tight like a spring.

Up till now, I've always had a minder who's helped control the crowds. But not here. It's too loud, disorderly, and chaotic. Family friends want me to come to dinner. A TV crew wants me to give an interview. Strangers congratulate me on my bravery and thank me for my service. I can't keep track of who's touching, patting, grasping. There's no order, no space, no room to breathe.

Aurora slides between me and the crowd. She must feel the tension in my body, the tightness with which I clutch her waist. She tugs at Dad's sleeve, stretches up on her toes, and whispers in his ear.

Dad's forehead bunches, and he turns to the crowd. "Okay, everyone, thanks for being here. Jake's delighted that you've all come out to welcome him. But let's give him some room, okay? It's been a long trip and he's tired. He'll be home all week and I'm sure he'll make time to see all of you, but right now he needs to get—"

"Now, just a minute!" the General gruffly interrupts. "These people have given up part of their day to come out and stand here in the hot sun. The least they deserve is a few words from our conquering hero."

Damn!

* * *

What is a hero? I'd say that it's just about anyone who ever served in the military. Probably anyone who's ever gone to war. Definitely anyone who's spent more than a day at Forward Operating Base Choke Point, running for the bunkers every time the warning siren wailed and soldiers shouted, "Incoming!"

"*Ahhhhhhhhhhh!*" In the dusty dimness, my buddy Skitballs hugged his knees and let out a shriek that made us all jump. With the sirens blaring, we'd all just dived into this bunker. Skitballs—Jayden Skinner, dark-skinned, tall, lanky—was the last guy in. He'd barely gotten here when the first missile blast slammed the reinforced door shut behind him. Had he been a second slower, there'd probably only be bits and pieces of him now.

"Y'all okay, Skits?" Morpiss asked in the near dark.

The stream of curses Skitballs unleashed were strangely reassuring. It sounded more like the grunt we knew, the dude who signed up so he could pay off his girlfriend's credit card debt with the enlistment bonus. We waited while he calmed down, taking deep breaths, his fists clenching and unclenching. "Goddamn!" he groaned. "What kind of psycho bat whack is this? Incoming day and night. Can't sleep. Can't think straight. Am I the only one here going crazy?"

We all were. Skitballs was just the first to say it out loud.

"Go see the doc. He'll give you something," a voice came from the shadows deeper in the bunker. From an older, grizzled, sunbaked guy wearing corporal stripes.

Looked too old to be a noncommissioned officer. But they said life in a war zone aged you in dog years.

"Give me something?" Skitballs asked. "Like what?"

He'd soon find out. We all would.

Retired Major General Windborne (Windy) Granger is my grandfather, my mother's father, and a famous war hero. Around Franklin they call him the General, and he still expects everyone to follow his orders. For the most part, they do.

Standing in the hot sun on the airport tarmac, the crowd grows quiet. One of the stupidest things I ever read was about how some people fear public speaking more than death. Anyone who believes that hasn't come within a thousand yards of a lead slug traveling 1,700 miles per hour straight for your face. Give a soldier a choice between standing before a crowd of a hundred thousand and telling them about the five most embarrassing things that ever happened to him, or being in a Humvee rolling over an IED—improvised explosive device—loaded with eighty pounds of potassium chlorate? I guarantee you he'll gladly tell the whole crowd about that time his sister walked into the bathroom while he was busy getting to know Mary Five-Fingers.

With the General beside me, I give the crowd what he wants: "Thank you all for coming out to greet me. I feel honored that you took the time. I hope you've seen on TV or the internet, me saying how proud I am to be from

Franklin, where people have big hearts and strong values. It's really good to be home."

The crowd cheers until the General raises a hand and quiets them so he can also thank them for coming out (and remind them that he's the hero's grandfather). Then it's over. Dad takes my arm and guides me toward the General's big black Mercedes. Not many people around Franklin would be allowed to bring their cars onto the airport runway, but guess which famous retired general can?

Before we get to the car, Sam Washington plants himself in front of me. He's wearing his Junior Reserve Officers Training Corps instructor uniform with all the fruit salad. He's a Gulf War vet and was my JROTC instructor at Franklin High. Probably around fifty years old and still in top military shape. He pulls me into a bear hug, crutches and all. With his lips close to my ear, he whispers, "You okay, son?"

Here's how I *wish* I could answer: by telling him to go to hell.

Here's how I do answer: "Yessir."

Sam lets me out of the hug but holds me at arm's length. "So you'll come speak to the class tomorrow," he says loud enough for those around us to hear. "They all want to hear your story."

What story will I tell them?

He lets go, but there's someone behind him. She's wearing a baggy gray athletic T and cutoffs, and her brown hair is gathered up in a loose bun of dreadlocks spreading out like octopus tentacles. "Hi, I'm Brandi," she says with a bright smile. Her gray-green eyes are piercing. "I've been texting you? You haven't answered, probably because you get so many."

Near us, the General makes no attempt to hide his glower. Is he offended that she's dressed so informally (in his mind: disrespectfully) for this event? Or is the explanation both simpler and uglier: that she's not the "correct" color?

"I'm from the *Franklin Frontier*," Brandi goes on, undeterred. "I know you've already given, like, a thousand interviews, but it would be so great if you'd give one to your former high school."

"I'm sorry, miss," the General harrumphs. "Jake's just come an awful long way. Now isn't the—"

"Oh, I didn't mean now." When Brandi cuts him short, my grandfather's eyes narrow and his jaw goes tight. Interrupting is something you just don't do to the General. The funny thing is, I get the feeling she knows this. Or at least senses it. And she cut in anyway.

"Maybe tomorrow?" Brandi says. "At school? After the JROTC class?"

"Sure," I tell her, pretending not to notice my grandfather's frown.

The General's driver holds the Mercedes's door open. A driver and car is one of the retirement perks some generals get. Now that I've gotten this close to Aurora, I hate to leave her again. But she understands. I give her a kiss and tell her I'll see her later. Inside the car, I have to ride in front because that's the only seat with enough legroom for my cast. Lori, Dad, and the General sit in the back.

When the Mercedes starts to move, my hands automatically slide toward my chest before I catch myself and place them in my lap. It's just muscle memory. The first time I rode in a Humvee with Brad, he told me to keep my hands inside my armor. I slid them through the arm holes, where they naturally landed on my pecs. I sat that way for a while, but my hands began to get hot and it felt weird to have them over my pecs anyway. So I took them out. Brad's eyes slid in my direction. I could see he disapproved.

About a month later a suicide bomber in an old car loaded with explosives rammed a Humvee just outside the wire and blew the guys inside to smithereens. Romeo Squad was on security detail that day, and Brad lined us up for casualty collection. His eyes went right past me, then stopped and returned as if he'd remembered something. "And especially you, Liddell. Go out and find the pieces. All of them."

He wasn't talking about pieces of the Humvee.

It was probably one of the worst things I ever had to do. One of the many chores you won't see in any Army recruiting commercial. Morpiss and I puked. A couple of other guys couldn't even do it. And, of course, as if Brad had known, there was a hand.

Now, in the privacy of the Mercedes, Lori wants to see *my* hand, which, luckily, is still attached to my body.

I drape my left arm over the seat. My hand is missing the pinkie and the distal phalanx of the ring finger. I hear a loud sniff. Lori starts to cry. I look back and my eyes meet Dad's. I wonder if he's thinking what I'm thinking. Losing a finger is nothing compared to what others have lost. I'd give my whole left arm if it meant Morpiss could get back half of what he's lost.

And Skitballs.

And Clay.

For what?

"You okay?" Dad asks.

"Of course he's okay," the General says. "He's a goddamn war hero."

THE GENERAL

The General was a corporal in Vietnam. His squad was ambushed in the jungle and the squad leader killed. My grandfather took command, broke the team in two, and ordered a fire-and-maneuver retreat to a point where they hoped to link up with reinforcements. The skirmish was fierce and, at times, hand-to-hand. Despite being wounded in the shoulder and arm, my grandfather never quit. After the squad linked up with the reinforcements and turned the retreat into an assault, he kept fighting and refused medical treatment until it was over.

They awarded him the Bronze Star. I wonder if he felt as weird about what happened then as I feel now. No, not a chance. He's always been gung-ho.

Guess I was like that once.

Not anymore.

The Army brass is still in the process of deciding what level of valor medal I'll be awarded. I've heard that they're considering me for the Silver Star. One step up from the bronze, one level higher than the General's.

Would I dare refuse it?

On the way home from the airport the signs in front of the fast-food places, the car wash, and the elementary school all say, WELCOME HOME, JAKE LIDDELL, OUR HERO.

At our house a silver-gray Jeep Wrangler in the driveway sparkles in the sunlight. I haven't heard anything about Dad or Lori getting a new car. The garage doors are open and inside are Dad's Cherokee and Lori's Honda.

The Mercedes stops behind the Wrangler. The Jeep's tail reflectors have that new-car shimmer.

No one gets out. I feel the General's hand clap my shoulder from behind. "You've earned it, son."

Is he serious?

We pile out. The Jeep's got that straight-from-the-showroom smell. I'm overwhelmed. From the time Lori and I were little, Dad made it clear that we weren't one of those families where the kids got everything they wanted. Some kids in our neighborhood were given cars as soon as they were old enough to drive. We were given advice on how to find a good used vehicle that we could afford with our savings.

"You don't have to do this, sir," I tell the General. I'd hug him, but he hates being hugged almost as much as he hates being called "Grandpa." So instead I endure another one of his bone-crushing handshakes.

"You deserve it," he says. "You're a real military man now."

It's no accident that he says this in front of my father, who, through no fault of his own, has spent his military career as a PowerPoint Ranger. Dad's a lieutenant colonel at the base here in Franklin, and the General never misses an opportunity to remind him that all he's ever been is a desk jockey. He's never gone to war; never tasted battle the way "real" soldiers do.

The General checks his watch. "I'll let you get some R and R." He heads back to the Mercedes, where his driver is holding the door. And then he's gone.

Dad, Lori, and I stay in the driveway with the new Jeep. It's completely unnecessary . . . and if I work up the guts to do what I believe I should do, I won't be the only one who feels that way. *Sure hope the General kept the receipt.*

I glance at Lori. She's two years older than me, so we've always had a brother/sister competition over who got what. But when my eyes meet hers, there's not a trace of resentment.

"You do deserve it," she says.

For a moment, I can't hold her gaze, and have to look away. When our eyes meet again, she's frowning as if she can sense that something's wrong.

"All right." Dad claps his hands. "Let's get you inside and settled."

Blue greets me at the front door with tentative sniffs. I rub his head and he wags his tail a little, but it's not the wag I'd get if he remembered me.

"He's so old." Lori tries to soften the blow. "All he does is sleep."

Blue's all gray around the muzzle, and he has those lumps under his coat that some old dogs get. He finishes sniffing and wanders slowly and stiffly off. I feel a pang. Not because he's gotten so old. But because seeing him reminds me of something else they don't show you in the ads for today's Army—how, over there, we had standing orders to shoot Blue's canine relatives on sight.

There were packs of wild dogs everywhere. Bony, mangy, terrible-looking creatures. And because we were not just there to fight an enemy, but to gain the trust of the local population, we were ordered to kill them.

Why? To show respect. To prove to the locals that we cared.

You only had to witness once what those starving dogs did to the bodies of the dead. Then you'd understand.

"What's this?" I'm standing in the doorway to the den. The chairs and couch have been pushed aside and a hospital bed dominates the room.

"We weren't sure how you'd do with the steps," Dad says.

On the floor are two large plastic United States Postal Service mail crates filled with letters and cards.

"Someone published our address on the internet," Lori explains.

A manila envelope lies on the hospital bed. It's got no

address or stamp. I open it. Inside are a dozen sheets of paper with names and phone numbers.

"And our phone number," Lori says. "These are the people who called."

I can't believe what I'm looking at. It's a spreadsheet that goes on for pages and pages. Hundreds of names and numbers. "You compiled this?"

"The message box kept filling up," she says. "So I'd transfer the names and numbers and empty it."

She didn't have to do that, but she knows it's what Mom would have done. Not returning calls is bad manners. Ever since Mom died of cancer six years ago, Lori's been half mother and half sister, and one of the few people I can talk to about practically everything.

Dad has to make a call and when Blue barks, Lori takes him out to the backyard. I'm left in the den. Getting this hospital bed was a thoughtful gesture, but there's no way I'm going to stay down here and be a spectacle everyone sees when they come and go. So I head for my room. Climbing the stairs in a full-leg cast isn't easy. If the handrail isn't securely anchored, you can accidentally pull it off the wall. That happened a few days ago outside the green room at a television station in New York City. Part of the rail came right out of the drywall. Fortunately, a production assistant caught me before I did a face-plant.

But this house is old and well built. The stairway rail is solidly anchored. I hobble up the steps.

My room hasn't changed. Same posters and furniture.

Same books and dumb trophies you get in sports just for showing up. The only thing that's different is the person who'll sleep here tonight.

I take out my phone and text Erin Rose: **Home. Need 2 C U. Important. Hit me back, K?**

I emailed her while I was over there. She didn't email back. I sent texts. She didn't answer. There are things she needs to know about Brad. Things I've absolutely promised myself to tell her face-to-face.

I toss the phone on the bed, slide my hands under the cast, and heave it up so I can lie down. Stare at the spidery cracks in the ceiling.

The last time I lay on this bed and stared at those cracks was early on the morning that I entered the Army. A little more than a year ago. Outside, the sun was still low and orange behind the trees. I lay here trying to will myself to go back to sleep, knowing I had a long day ahead. I'd only gone to bed a few hours earlier. But I was wide-awake. Couldn't wait until it was time to go. Couldn't wait to get on that bus to Fort Benning. I knew boot camp was going to be tough, but I'd gotten a head start on the Army Physical Fitness Test. I'd been doing the pyramid workout, cutting back on calories, trying, not very successfully, to change my sleep schedule.

When my phone chimed that morning, I figured it was Aurora getting an early start on our last few hours together. But the voice on the other end of the line was from Mortuary Affairs, asking if I wanted to be buried or cremated? Did I know the name and location of the cemetery? What type of headstone? What scripture? What personal effects did I want to be buried with? Did I have a preference for the music that would be played?

I remember thinking that it was about the worst welcome imaginable to the armed forces. Now I think it's just the military's way of preparing you for what you're going to spend practically every day of your deployment thinking about.

Now here I am again, a year later, on this bed. I'm glad to be home with my family and Aurora, glad to be in a place where enemy rockets don't come screaming in day and night. But I miss my buddies. I miss the weighty reassurance of my rifle on my lap, miss the friendship, the joshing and joking, and even the shared terror. The camaraderie. Morpiss, Skitballs, Magnet, Clay.

Brad . . .

BRAD

Out in the dark, someone was going bonkers on a drum kit. It was my first night at Forward Operating Base Choke Point and the last thing I imagined hearing. I was walking around after dinner, trying to get a feel for the place. The FOB was surrounded by a HESCO barrier, a wall of dirt maybe six feet thick. Beyond that were sand berms and razor wire. Not much was going to get through on foot. Inside the FOB were barracks, the DFAC (dining facility), PX (base store where you could buy candy, cigarettes, and Rip It), and assorted offices and storage in Conex boxes. In the far north corner of the FOB were vehicle sanitation and the boneyard where "blowed-up" vehicles were towed. I would soon learn that no one at the FOB ever said "blown-up."

It was near the boneyard that I discovered the square of sandbags, rising up about six feet on all sides. The space inside must have been just large enough for a drum set. For a moment I wondered if it was a PSYOP thing. I'd heard that Army psychological operations liked to blast enemy combatants with heavy metal music like "Back in Black" and "Enter Sandman." It was said that doing so drove the enemy crazy and provoked spontaneous, and usually suicidal, one-man attacks.

But what I was hearing that night was just loud manic drumming without accompaniment. I found the opening and looked in. There was Brad. Shirt off, body glistening with sweat in the moonlight. Going gaga on the skins. And the funny thing was, even though it was dark, I knew it was him. Because I'd heard him play back home.

I watched and listened. When he gave no indication of letting up, I stepped in front of the bass drum, feeling the sonic booms. . . . It might just as well have been blasts of artillery. Brad kept pounding like a man possessed. For a few moments, he still didn't see me.

Then he did.

He stopped. He blinked as if he thought his eyes must have been playing tricks on him. Breathing hard, he wiped the sweat off his face with a T-shirt. Finally, he snorted. "What are the odds?"

Brad was from Franklin. We'd gone to the same high school.

We'd been in love with the same girl.

Her name was Erin Rose. She and I started going together in sixth grade. What did we know about relationships?

Well, maybe Erin Rose knew something, but I sure didn't. With a smirk, Lori called it "puppy love."

By eighth grade, Erin Rose was a knockout. She'd matured early the way some girls do. People were always telling her to enter beauty contests, but she thought they were stupid. Every guy I knew was jealous of me.

Brad was a junior. He drove a Vette and played drums with the Zombie Horde, a local heavy metal band that didn't mind turning down the volume to play at weddings and school dances. Sometime during the spring of eighth grade, Erin Rose caught his eye. Looking back now, it's obvious that I didn't stand a chance. But at the time I was heartbroken.

Brad and Erin Rose got serious really fast. By the time he enlisted after graduation, Erin Rose (then going into tenth grade) was pregnant. Brad had done four years of JROTC at Franklin High and entered basic training as an E-3, which meant better pay than someone who walked in off the street and signed up. It also meant that if he did four years in the service, he'd be eligible for a college scholarship, even though the only college that would have interested Brad was the University of Heavy Metal.

The day before he went into the Army, he gave Erin Rose an engagement ring. Their daughter, Amber, was born at the end of sophomore year. Since Franklin High provides daycare, Erin Rose came back for junior year. Brad was home from his first deployment by then. Sometimes I'd see him drop Erin Rose and Amber at school in the morning.

At the end of Erin Rose's and my junior year, Brad redeployed. I heard rumors that Erin Rose was furious about him leaving Amber. Then, sometime during our senior year, she and I patched things up and became friends. I guess part of the reason was that we'd shared so much in middle school. Another part was probably whatever had attracted us to each other in the first place. But when Brad found out we were hanging around, he became crazy jealous. I guess it was understandable. He was on his second deployment, over there where the only available females were camels and goats.

The truth was, he had nothing to worry about. Erin Rose wasn't that kind of girl, and by then I'd started dating Aurora. But Brad couldn't relax about it. I guess a little part of me enjoyed knowing it drove him crazy. Like it was revenge.

And now here we were, assigned to the same FOB thousands of miles from home. Like Brad said, what were the odds?

He flipped a drumstick up into the dark night air and caught it. "So, Private, may I ask what Windy Granger's grandson is doing in this hellhole?"

"Signed up, sir."

"I think you mean, Staff Sergeant Burrows," Brad corrected me. "I work for a living."

I snapped to attention. "Staff Sergeant Burrows, sorry."

"At ease, Private." He frowned. "You enlisted? Why?"

"I didn't want to take the easy route, Staff Sergeant."

When he grinned, his teeth were white in the

moonlight. "Man, you are even stupider than I thought."

It was my first night at the FOB. The first time I'd seen Brad in years. This wasn't the time or place to go into an in-depth explanation for why I'd enlisted. Anyway, at that moment I had a much more pressing concern. "May I ask a favor, Staff Sergeant?"

"Go ahead, Private."

"Staff Sergeant, I truly hope that no one will find out about the General. I worry that it would really mess things up for me here."

Sitting behind the drum kit, Brad twirled a stick around his finger. I couldn't think of a good reason why he should have granted my request. It wasn't like I was going to add, "It's the least you can do, considering you stole my girlfriend." But I was worried that if word got out about who my grandfather was, my sorry grunt butt would be razzed raw for my entire deployment.

Brad knew he had me by the nuts, at least for the next eight to twelve months. He tilted his head back and looked up into the black, star-speckled sky. Then he started to bash the skins again.

ALJAHIM

J *ake! I'm hit!"* Skitballs is screaming.

I've tucked myself into the twisted wreckage of the Humvee, where I'm protected by the truck's body and an open door. Bullets are whizzing and snapping everywhere. From the searing hot burning points in my legs, back, and left arm, I know I've taken a lot of shrapnel. The pain is bad, but not immobilizing.

Up and down the road are thick black plumes of smoke. The IEDs that blew up our convoy must have been daisy-chained. A hundred yards of bombs had gone off just when the convoy was directly over them. The insurgents were already dug in and waiting to pick off any of our guys who were lucky enough to survive the blasts.

"Jake!" Skitballs screams again. Other than a general direction, I can't figure out where he is. Can't lift my head to look for him without getting it blown off. But wherever he is, it's a cinch he's out of the line of enemy fire.

Otherwise, he'd have been smoked by now.

"Clay! Magnet!" I call out to the other guys.

Shots rip through the air. The firefight is kinetic. Gunfire feels like it's coming from all directions. Whoever is shooting on our side is keeping the insurgents from getting closer. The most intense fire is coming from my right, from behind a pockmarked wall with vaulted openings that line the road.

"Oh lord, Jake!" Skitballs screams.

"Clay! Magnet!" I shout as loud as I can. No answer. Crude animal logic kicks in. I can't get to Skitballs as long as the enemy is firing from behind that wall. So I have to eliminate them first. I throw a flashbang over the wall, then jump up and hustle through the closest opening. The pain from my wounds slows me, but I'm totally juiced on adrenaline. There are two shooters in the small courtyard where I threw the flashbang. One is curled on his side, his eyes squeezed shut and his hands over his ears. The other one is on his hands and knees, blinking as he gropes for the AK on the dusty ground a few feet away.

I shoot him first, then aim at the other guy. Do you shoot a defenseless man lying curled on the ground? A few seconds ago he'd been trying to kill me. And in a few moments from now, when he's reoriented, he'll want to try again.

I pull the trigger. In boot camp, they teach you about the Geneva Conventions and the proper conduct of combat under the code of military war. None of that means doodly-squat when it's either you or him. Right now anyone who's still alive from our convoy isn't fighting for America. We're not making a stand for democracy or freedom. We're just a bunch of scared nineteen- and twenty-year-olds doing whatever we can to stay alive.

Something smacks into me from behind and knocks me flat on my face. It felt like a sledgehammer. I roll onto my back, expecting to find an attacker.

There's just the empty courtyard and blue sky above.

Whap! A round slams into the ground inches from my head, kicking dirt into my eyes. Now I know what hit me in the back. A sniper round. Thank Almighty God and ceramic body armor. So where's the shooter? Probably on a roof.

I start to roll. *Whap!* The next round smacks into the ground exactly where my head was an instant ago.

I roll into shade. The shots stop. I'm under a veranda. Out of the sun and out of the sights of the sniper.

He has to assume he hasn't gotten me.

I have to assume he's coming to finish the job.

BRAD

FOB Choke Point sat on a bluff overlooking a valley that connected two enemy provinces. With us perched there, the insurgents were forced to move men and equipment through the surrounding mountains—a much tougher and slower way to go. To show their displeasure with us for blocking their valley, hardly a day passed that they didn't lob a dozen rockets in our direction.

Thus, the first thing you learned at the FOB was where the bunkers were. The good news was there were plenty of them, all dug deep and fortified. Day or night, sirens and shouts of "Incoming!" meant diving for the closest bunker.

Those first few weeks, while the new recruits walked around with a constant knot in their stomachs, waiting for the next enemy rocket, I had two knots in mine. Every time someone looked at me funny or smirked, I immediately assumed the worst—that Brad had spread the word about who my grandfather was. But it turned out I was mistaken. Brad never told a soul.

We stayed out of each other's way. Not that we never saw each other. The FOB wasn't that big, and everyone ate in the chow hall and hung around the rec center. And, of course, I could always hear when he was drumming. When guys needed to blow off steam, they could pump iron and exercise. They could play basketball. Or they could go beat the hell out of those drums.

On my "hero tour" here in the States, when interviewers asked me what the Army did to make life in the war zone bearable, I told them how we had real beds with mattresses, not cots. How the diesel generators were strong enough to provide air-conditioning even on days when the temperatures got to 120. How sometimes on Sundays we had steak at dinner and ice cream afterward.

I didn't tell them about the pills, nor about the night I was in the rec room shooting pool and Brad charged in half-whacked out of his mind and went nose to nose with me. As active-duty soldiers, we weren't allowed to drink or do any drug the docs hadn't handed out themselves. But the meds the docs had were potent, and it was obvious to everyone that Brad was totally amped. It wasn't alcohol or I would have smelled it on his breath. Besides, he was wired, not sloppy. His eyes were wild, his face red, and he was breathing hard and sweating as if he'd just spent an hour hitting the skins.

Only I hadn't heard any drums that night.

"You touch her while I was gone?" he screamed. The whole rec hall went quiet. I wiped the odd bits of spit off my face and wondered if Brad knew that he was clenching and unclenching his fists. Next, I checked to make sure he wasn't armed. Then I leaned back, my hand resting on the cue lying on the pool table behind me. Good thing there were plenty of soldiers around because if I had to smack him upside the head, I'd need witnesses to testify that it was self-defense.

"Well?" he demanded. His face couldn't have been any redder. I couldn't imagine where this craziness had come from. I'd been at the FOB for a month and, after that first night by the drum set, we'd hardly said a word to each other.

"Staff Sergeant Burrows, no," I said calmly.

"You *sure?*"

"Yes, Staff Sergeant."

"What if I told you I heard something?"

That threw me for an instant. Then I reminded myself that it was all in his head. "Then somebody lied, Staff Sergeant."

He glared at me, still sucking air like he'd run the hundred in twelve flat. I stared right back. In the past month, he'd made it pretty clear that he wasn't going to tell anyone about my vaunted military family. I appreciated that. But I'd also just come through basic training. So it was going to take a little more than one half-mental unarmed NCO to unnerve me.

LORI

We can take it if you want," Lori says. We're in the driveway, beside the new Jeep. She has to give me a ride to Franklin High, since, with the cast, I can't drive myself.

I shake my head. Don't want to risk dinging the Jeep when it may be on its way back to the dealership soon.

Lori gives me a look. "Isn't this the car you've always dreamed of?"

"Yup."

"So?"

When I shrug, she narrows her eyes. "There's something you're not telling me, Jake."

I haven't had an opportunity to tell her what I'm thinking about doing. But it looks like the time has come. "We'll take your car. I'll tell you on the way."

MR. WASHINGTON

What's it like over there?"

It's the question I've been dreading. I am seated in front of the JROTC class. Mr. Washington is standing by the door, in uniform, military erect, at parade rest. The kids in the class sit up straight, wearing their uniforms. There is no class in school with better posture. A year ago I was one of these kids.

It's one thing when the interviewers ask what it's like over there. I can give them the standard replies. It's tough, but we're making progress. I'm proud that we're one of the countries that is standing up to the threat.

But in this class are the kids who may go over there next. I'm only a year older than some of them, but they look so young. I scan these bright, interested faces. Some with zits. Some haven't even started shaving. *Which of you will still be alive a year from now? Which of you will still have all four limbs?*

Which of you will have been shipped home in a flag-covered coffin?

Mr. Washington is watching me, waiting for my reply to the question. Mr. Washington, who once took me aside and said confidently that my future in the military "was boundless." That someday I could be a major general just like my famous grandfather.

I'll bet almost every kid in this class plans to enlist just like I did. Why? Because someone has to stop the radical extremists who want to kill everyone who disagrees with their totally warped worldview. I haven't seen the numbers of troops each country has sent to the conflict, but it's called a "US-led coalition." I have a sneaking suspicion that means that most of the troops over there are Americans. As has been the case so often in history, once again it's mostly left to the US to do the dirty work. And how do we do that? With a military force made up of innocent kids who don't have a clue what they're getting themselves into.

But it has to be this way, doesn't it? Because if these kids really knew what they were signing up for, they wouldn't enlist. And if they don't enlist, then we don't have an army. And if we don't have an army, the bad guys win.

The class is waiting. *Come on, Jake, what's it like over there?*

We lived every minute at FOB Choke Point knowing it might be our last. All you had to do was be in the wrong place at the wrong time when a Chinese- or Russian-made rocket smashed in. You just had to hope you'd be one of the lucky ones. Like Magnet, who got his nickname because wherever he went, he seemed to attract incoming. One time he was in the crapper and a dud mortar round blew through the roof and crashed into the toilet across from him. Shattered the thing into a thousand pieces.

After that, if you passed the crapper and saw a line of guys outside holding their nuts like they were going to piss themselves any second, you knew Magnet was inside. No one dared go in when he was there.

Every time we left the FOB, we knew it might be the last time. We all had good luck charms. Some soldiers smoked, some joked, some dipped and spat, and some got on their knees and prayed. By the time we'd been there three months, more than a few guys were taking pills for sleeplessness, loose bowels, and anxiety.

The pills for pain, depression, and night terrors would come later.

We were trained for asymmetric warfare. Around the FOB they called it a 360-degree 3-D war. Not like the old wars with front lines, and you knew that the enemy was on the other side of that line. Not even like what I'd heard about Nam, with its jungle warfare. This war is like being inside a sphere of terror. You go into a town and insurgents can shoot at you from anywhere and everywhere. From doorways and windows and rooftops. Mortar rounds fall from above; IEDs blow up from below. Because there is no front line, there is no clear direction toward safety.

At my first Sunday service at FOB Choke Point, the chaplain asked us if we were prepared to die. He said if we weren't, we had better get prepared fast. Not a day passed that you didn't imagine how it might happen. The rocket blast. The sniper bullet. The IED. The mortar round. The RPG. The shot in the head that's instant lights-out. The shot in the groin that slowly bleeds out. The supersonic shrapnel that rips off a leg, an arm, a head. The thirty-pound artillery shell that leaves nothing but pink mist.

All we could do was tell ourselves it wouldn't be us. It would be someone else. But soldiers got shot or "blowed up" all the time. Some were horribly wounded. Some died. And why wouldn't it be one of us? Can there be good luck without bad luck?

And then it was one of us: Morpiss.

And then it was more of us.

Until there was hardly anyone left.

The sound of Mr. Washington clearing his throat brings me back to the classroom. Back to these straight-backed, pink-cheeked, eager kids who can't wait to enter whatever noble fantasy they have of what war is.

So what's it like?

Here's what I can't say: You won't be over there long before you'll realize that war isn't what you imagined it would be. Before you'll wish to God that you'd never come. Before you'll lie in bed at night so scared and trembling and sick with fear that you'll be a hair's width from bawling loudly for your mommy.

Maybe you'll be one of the ones who does break down. Or snaps. Or goes Section 8.

Why? Because you're going to see horrible things. The vehicle filled with your buddies is going to blow up right before your eyes. Men in flames are going to try to run, but they won't get far before a triggerman or the fire snuffs them. You will see blood spurting from stumps where legs or arms or heads were an instant before. You will see children die. That's something else the Army "forgets" to prepare you for during basic. They show you how to shoot at targets. They show you how to throw grenades at pretend mortar positions. They don't show you what the body of a mangled, bloody child looks like.

Some of you are going to wish to God that you never took this JROTC class instead of gym.

"It's . . . it's hard," I hear myself say. "It's war. It can be really scary. But someone has to do it."

I glance over at Mr. Washington, who nods approvingly. When I was a student here, that approving nod from my instructor was what I yearned for. Before becoming a JROTC instructor, Mr. Washington had been the commander of a five-ton gun truck in Iraq, armed front and back with .50 caliber machine guns. His job was to escort convoys.

He told us that he'd encountered plenty of small arms and sniper fire. It sounded so cool. Protecting convoys. Actually exchanging fire with the enemy.

It wasn't until I got over there that I learned how limited my JROTC instructor's experience had actually been. The convoys he'd guarded had stayed on roads far from insurgent-infested villages. And he'd been protected inside a heavily armored vehicle. Whatever fire he'd exchanged with the enemy had been from a distance. Far enough that I doubt he could ever say for certain that he'd had a confirmed kill.

In the JROTC classroom, the questions keep coming. I tread a fine line with my answers. I don't want to bad-mouth the military, but I also can't leave here thinking that I've been encouraging. Anyone who feels encouraged and enlists after graduation could be dead in six months.

I can't have their blood on my hands. I've already got enough to last a lifetime.

Relief floods through me when the bell finally rings. One more obligation satisfied. One less albatross around my neck. One step closer to salvation.

The kids file out of the classroom. Some thank me for speaking to them. Some just look awestruck. They stare at my cast and the scar on my chin. Some try to sneak a peek at my disfigured hand.

Then it's just Mr. Washington and me. My stomach clenches for an instant with that old impulse to please. Then I remind myself of where I've been for the past six months. I'm the one who's experienced war up close and personal. I'm the supposed hero.

"Sorry you had a tough time, Jake." Mr. Washington puts a hand on my shoulder. "We're all proud of you."

I serve up a grim smile, and at the same time fight off

the sudden jolt of anger that wants to tell him precisely where he can go. I have to clench my fists and take a deep breath. Mr. Washington is just one small step up from all those strangers who thank me for my service without having any idea what that means. People who have good intentions, but can't comprehend that in so many cases "service" means that if you're not dead, you're physically and psychologically crippled for life. It means you will never, ever be the same. At least Mr. Washington fought, even if it was in a limited way. But I doubt he's known anyone who's been through what Romeo Squad experienced.

Why? Because if he really knew what I've been through, he wouldn't be teaching JROTC. He'd be telling kids to stay as far away from the military as possible.

We shake hands, and he thanks me for coming in. That sudden bolt of anger has left me feeling shaky and lightheaded. These blasts of seething resentment are easily triggered, and I'm not always prepared for them. Out in the hall, the second bell has rung and the kids are in class. I'm alone. Just walls of blue lockers and wooden classroom doors. The squish of my crutches' rubber tips on the floor. The swish of my left foot sliding across the tiles.

The anger over what happened to me and my squad. The burden of having to live up to everyone else's idea of what it is to be a hero. It's draining and wearying. This hallway isn't the only thing that feels empty.

BRANDI

H ow are you?" asks Brandi, the reporter for the *Franklin Frontier*, the high school's online newspaper. We're in a small glassed-in room in the high school library. "I mean, after *five* operations?"

"I'm . . . okay." The question catches me off-guard. I've given dozens of interviews in the past few weeks, but not many of the interviewers knew how many surgeries I underwent at Landstuhl. Brandi's done her homework.

She looks different. No baggy athletic T and cutoffs today. She's wearing tight jeans and a designer T-shirt that doesn't leave much to the imagination. Her long dark hair now falls in ringlets past her shoulders. Makeup enhances those penetrating hazel eyes. After nearly a year in which I've had very little contact with any female not wearing desert boots and body armor . . . Let's just say that, in Brandi's presence, my thoughts keep wanting to veer into inappropriate territory.

"You seemed to hesitate," she says.

I rap my knuckles against the cast. "Still recovering."

"What do you *really* think of the war?" she asks in the way of people who don't think much of it.

Nearly every interviewer has been respectful and sympathetic. This morning, at the local Franklin TV station, the interviewer fawned over me. Then again, Franklin is a military town. The Army base is the largest employer. When it comes to all things armed services, the local residents are gung-ho.

It's sort of ironic that I had to wait until a high school interview to be given a hard time. "No beating around the bush, huh?" I joke.

She smiles thinly. "Want me to lob a softball? How does it feel to be a hero, Jake? Are you happy to be home again? Did you miss home cooking?"

Her tone is almost caustic.

"You against us being over there?" I ask.

She sits back and lets out a sigh. "No, not entirely. I just . . . Honestly, Jake, does it feel like we're making any progress?"

Interesting. Half the "professional" TV interviewers were content to ask what it felt like to be a hero? (I'm still not sure.) Was I scared? (Hell, yes.) Did I ever think I was going to die? (Constantly, and with good reason.)

But that's the thing. Ever since the ambush, I've had too much time to think. Lying in hospital beds. Flying around in everything from big C-130 transports to tiny four-seat prop planes. Sitting in the backs of cars. All I did was think. Are we making progress? If progress is sacrificing young American lives over there so that people don't die here, then maybe we are. And since I am a member of the military, part of me feels obligated to give the answer that's expected. But another, more private part asks, what about Brad, and Morpiss, and Skitballs? What about all these young men and women who enlisted with valor in their eyes and duty and honor in their hearts (not to mention big enlistment bonuses in their pockets)? Now dead or forever maimed. Who's asking them if they think it was worth it?

What good is an enlistment bonus if you're not around to spend it?

The longer Brandi waits for my answer, the higher her carefully tweezed eyebrows rise.

"Guess I'm hesitating again, huh?" I ask.

Her eyes dart to the recording app on her phone.

"Yes, I do think we're making progress against the enemy." There it is—the official answer, the one I'm expected to make. *When are you going to make the statement you're not expected to make?*

Our eyes meet. I suspect that Brandi's penetrating gaze is asking . . . no, *saying*, that she has a hunch that the answer I've given is not what I really think. Just like Lori sensed this morning before she drove me here. I realize I'm being reckless. Brandi's hardly the first pretty and smart interviewer I've faced. Whatever it is about her that almost got me to drop my guard, I have to be more careful.

THE RECRUITER

H e sits at his table in the high school lobby, along with all the colorful pamphlets and Army Strong posters. He's not the same recruiter who signed me up. He's new, but doing the same job, coming here regularly, looking for fresh meat.

When I see him, I tell myself to keep going, that nothing I say will change anything. But Lori won't be back to pick me up for another fifteen minutes. I stop in front of the table. It's like I can't help myself. The recruiter is staring at his phone, but when he senses my presence, he looks up, sees my cast, frowns, then forces a smile.

"May I?" I gesture to the chair on the near side of the desk.

"Of course."

I sit. Instantly my thoughts are back to roughly a year ago, the last time I sat at this table. The day I signed up. The recruiter back then was a guy named Marshall. We'd been talking for weeks. The way Marshall described it, the Army was like a 24/7 college fraternity house, only better because you got a cash bonus to join, party, shoot guns, and collect a monthly paycheck.

This new recruiter nods at the cast. "How'd it happen?"

When I tell him my femur and ankle were shattered by rounds from an NSV heavy machine gun, his eyes widen. He figures it out. "Oh, I heard you might be coming here." He offers his hand. "It's an honor."

I should shake his hand. Whatever I'm royally ticked off about isn't his fault. He's just doing his job. But it's too late. The recruiter's hand hangs unmet in the air between us. Then he retracts it and starts to look tense and wary.

"What kind of bonuses are you offering these days?" I ask.

"Twenty thousand to quick ship. But you have to be ready to go in thirty days. Forty thousand if you sign up for four years."

Just as my feet brought me here of their own volition, now my mouth wants to go off on its own. Along with those sudden flashes of anger, my impulse control is out of whack. "That's serious scratch. You tell them about the eight years of inactive reserve after they get out?"

The recruiter squirms a little. Now he definitely looks uncomfortable.

I'm not finished: "The guy who used to sit here? He forgot to mention that when I signed up. Funny thing. Turned out most of the guys I served with were signed by recruiters who 'forgot.' They told one of my buddies he could quit any time he wanted by asking for a failure-to-adapt discharge. Can you believe it? And a bunch of guys got the line about the chances of seeing active duty being slim to none. And guess what? Two of them came home in a box."

The recruiter shoves his hands into his pockets and stares at the table. It's common knowledge that recruiters have to lie in order to make their quotas. (What happens if they don't make their quotas? Do they risk getting reassigned to even crappier jobs, like Mortuary Affairs? Imagine spending your days sifting through bags of body parts, trying to match them to the appropriate corpses.)

I lean forward. "Listen, man, I know they've got you between a rock and a hard place. You didn't ask for this job. And now that you've got it, you just want to do your time and get out."

He nods almost imperceptibly.

"But be honest with these kids, okay? They don't know anything except what they see on TV. Those ads about making a difference and being a problem solver? They don't have a clue about what really goes on over there."

The recruiter taps his fingers on his laptop, which is filled with slick videos designed to convince new recruits that they're about to become superheroes. He knows everything I've said is true.

And he's not going to do a thing about it.

AURORA

We're meeting at TGI Fridays. Emily and Michael can't make it, but Emily wants us to come to the pool party after. . . ."

Aurora's in front of her mirror, trying on clothes. We're in the room she grew up in. In her parents' house because with car payments and student loans, she can't afford a place of her own. I'm sitting by the window. In the backyard next door, some kids are kicking a soccer ball around a freshly mown green lawn. How many times over there did I see kids playing soccer in some dusty street, surrounded by the crumbled concrete and twisted rebar of bombed-out buildings? And then a few days later I would see the same kids playing a different kind of game. Instead of a soccer ball, they'd be lugging rusty old AKs. Kids as young as nine and ten whose fathers had been killed or maimed in battle. Kids who now needed to make money to feed their families. The insurgents paid them twenty-five dollars a month to fight in a grown-ups' war.

"Jake?" Aurora is facing me, a couple of different colored tops draped over her arm. "Did you hear what I said?"

"About swimming?"

"I asked if you brought a bathing suit."

"What's the point?" I gesture at my cast.

"I just think you'll feel more comfortable."

I'm wearing long sleeves and pants. Except for the missing finger and the scar on my chin, she has no idea what my body looks like now. The scars and gashes from shrapnel and surgery. The entrance and exit wounds of the rounds that tore right through me. I don't have a clue what my leg will look like when this cast comes off. "I'll be fine like this."

Aurora leaves the small bedroom. Why do I feel relieved when she's not here? Because I'm not the same person I used to be. Does anyone come back from war the same person they were when they left? Maybe if you're a fobbit who never stepped outside the wire for your entire deployment.

She comes back wearing a pink top. She went into the bathroom to change. It's been nine months since we've been in close proximity. Even with all the Skyping, calls, and texts, there's an awkward shyness between us that wasn't there when I left. She knows some of what I've been through. I'm sure she's read up on wounded warriors, PTSD, on the high rate of returning soldier violence and suicide. Maybe she also senses that I'm not the same person. Maybe she feels like she doesn't know this "new" me.

I'm not sure I do either.

So she fills the unsettled space between us with words — about dental hygienist school, about Sue Ann's pregnancy and what color she wants to paint the nursery, about what Luke's mother said about Jen's weight, and how Trey's parents have offered to help buy them a home, but only if . . .

I'm thinking about Brandi. An hour ago she texted asking if we could meet again. She wants to show me something she's been working on. I'm recalling those piercing hazel eyes. And the quick intelligence behind them. What made her sense that I have doubts? What did she see? Am I not doing as good a job of hiding it as I thought? Maybe she's simply smart enough to know that it's natural to have doubts. She knows I've seen death up close, been seriously wounded, undergone all those operations. Makes sense I'd be somewhat less than gung-ho, right?

But what if it isn't a guess? What if she can see into me? Then, along with Lori, there are now two people who suspect I'm pretending to be something I'm not sure I want to be.

"Sue Ann thinks it's blackmail, and I agree. Trey's mom is going to be over there all the time, telling her how to decorate, what shrubs to plant, and—"

"Aurora!" Suddenly I can't take her blabbering.

She freezes, then stares wide-eyed, the way she'd stare at a snarling dog.

Damn it! Instantly I'm filled with regret. I've never snapped at her before. Prior to going over there, I never felt irritable or angry for no reason.

Aurora's still frozen in place, staring at me. She doesn't deserve to be snapped at. She is the sweetest, kindest, most thoughtful person I've ever known. Always thinking about others. Always there to help. There are three reasons I'm still alive: luck, the desire to survive, and Aurora.

I heave myself up and spread my arms. Whatever's going on inside me, it isn't her fault. "Hey, come here."

She approaches hesitantly. Like I'm that dog she isn't sure about. Now she's in my arms, her head nestled against my shoulder, the fragrance of her hair once again in my nose. "I'm sorry," I whisper.

"You're different, Jake." She sounds stung.

I can't deny it. These furies inside me boil up so fast and unexpectedly.

She slides her arms around my waist. "I know things must have happened. Things you don't want to tell me about."

She has no idea. No one does. Except, maybe, the General. In Nam, he was in firefights. He was wounded. But unlike me, it only seemed to make him more gung-ho military. How was that possible? How could he come through that without any PTSD? It's practically abnormal.

Aurora gives me a hug. "You're like Dr. Jekyll and Mr. Hyde."

I hug her back. "Dr. Jekyll and Private First Class Hyde."

She gives a tiny chuckle. For the moment, things are better.

* * *

Jen and Luke. Sue Ann and Trey. These are the couples Aurora and I hung around with back in the day. I haven't seen them since we graduated. At TGI Fridays we catch up. They tell me what they've been doing. But then there's that awkward moment when it's my turn. Aurora's probably warned them about my visible wounds. Maybe she's even suggested that they not ask me about what happened over there.

Another round of sodas and iced teas arrives. How's this for irony? I'm old enough to kill, old enough to have seen humans do unimaginably vicious and cruel things to one another. But not old enough to order a beer.

Trey brings up sports. Relief spreads around the table. Here's something we can talk about. Chatter about our favorite division one teams carries us until the cheese fries and fried shrimp appetizers arrive. Man, does this stuff taste good. At the FOB they tried their best. I've already mentioned the occasional Sunday steaks and ice cream. But then there were times when weather, or enemy maneuvers, or just plain military snafus made it impossible to resupply. We'd have a week of battery acid (coffee) with armored cow (condensed milk), dead donkey (canned ham), bug juice, and the four fingers of death (hot dogs). That was usually when Skitballs would come a little unglued and start going on stealth missions to liberate every pack of Skittles he could find in our MREs, the prepackaged ready-to-eat meals we carried on patrols. The FOB's rat and mouse population would suddenly triple as they feasted on the ripped-open MRE pouches he'd leave behind.

But I can't think of Skitballs without thinking about the ambush. And I can't think about the ambush without feeling a flood of pain and regret. And I can't feel that pain and regret without thinking of what I would do today if I were truly brave.

Aurora nudges me gently, bringing me back to dinner. So far I've managed to eat with my right hand. I've kept my left hand in my lap. I could probably continue to keep it hidden through the appetizer course, but what's the point? I'm sure they all know about it. So I pick up a napkin with both hands and dab my lips.

They all stare at my left hand for a moment. It's like they've been waiting. But it's probably not as bad as some of them have imagined. The Army surgeons did a pretty good job of smoothing the raggedness. It almost looks like I was simply born with three and two-thirds fingers on my left hand.

The entrees arrive. It's knife-and-fork time with both hands in use, but our friends are no longer watching. Conversationwise, there's the current baseball season to discuss, and next fall's football prospects. We chew over sports as thoroughly as we chew our New York strip steaks and baby back ribs.

By dessert, the subject of sports has been exhausted. We plow through our New York cheesecake and brownies with vanilla ice cream, and talk about cars, movies, what various people we graduated with are up to. Finally, the bill comes. We've made it through the entire meal without a single mention of the military. You'd think that after all those interviews it would be a relief not to have to talk about it. But strangely, I felt its absence.

At Emily's they set me up on a lounge at the pool's edge. This warm evening is filled with laughter, talk, splashing, and teasing. Out of the dark come the chirps and peeps of crickets and tree frogs. More importantly, out come beer, tequila, and spiced rum.

Aurora and my friends are careful not to leave me alone. There's always someone at the edge of the pool ready to chat. Someone with hair soaked and tanned skin dotted with drops. The smile on my face is sometimes authentic, sometimes forced. They're trying their best to make me feel comfortable while they have fun.

It's not their fault that I'm thinking about Skitballs again, lying wounded in an open sewer in the middle of the firefight. His bright red blood mixing with human waste.

Stop, Jake. No one made you enlist. It was your decision.

In the pool are the ones who chose not to enlist. With the exception of Aurora, all of them are at four-year colleges or universities now, still preparing to begin their careers. I must be the only one who feels like his career is probably over.

Emily swims over and rests her arms on the edge of the pool. They're all pretty girls, but she's the prettiest, with black hair and dark eyes and full lips. Her father used to be my pediatrician. She plans to become a radiologist. She just finished her freshman year at Barnard College in New York City.

"Sorry you can't come in," she says.

"One of these days."

"But aren't you leaving at the end of the week?"

"Yeah. They're shipping me to Walter Reed for rehab."

"And then?"

Good question. If she were reading an MRI of my heart, what would she see? What do I see?

"What makes you ask?" I'm curious.

She rakes her fingers through her slick wet hair and shakes it out. "Not sure. Just a feeling. After what you've been through? Like maybe you've paid your dues?"

"I haven't finished my deployment. There's still a war going on."

With a whoop, Luke does a cannonball off the diving board. Water sprays everywhere. Some even gets on me. Everyone cheers. Small waves splash against the sides of the pool.

"There'll always be a war going on," Emily says when the noise dies down. "I hear they call it the Forever War."

True that.

"How long do you think she'll wait?" Emily asks.

There's no question who she's talking about. I don't waste much time wondering if Aurora sent her on this mission. The answer is almost surely no. That's not the way

Aurora rolls. But Emily's always been one of her closest friends and doesn't hesitate to say what's on her mind.

"It's not like no one else is interested." Emily nods toward the snack table, where Aurora's talking to a guy wearing green board shorts. Normally, there's nothing that lifts my spirits more than seeing Aurora in a bikini. She's chatting and laughing with the guy, who's got a decent build and sun-streaked hair. And whose body isn't peppered with scars. You don't have to observe their body language for long to see that they're comfortable with each other. This isn't the first time they've chatted.

"Doug Rhinebach," Emily says.

"As in Rhinebach Ford?"

"Not anymore. Now it's the Rhinebach Auto *Group*. Ford, BMW, Honda, Jeep, and yadda yadda yadda. Don't get me wrong, Jake. Aurora's been true blue to you, but how much longer do you expect her to hold out?"

The moment's finally here. Aurora and I left the party and are parked in a secluded place. She's in my arms. Before we left Emily's, she took a quick shower. Her hair is damp and stringy, but she smells great and feels great. I've dreamed about this for a long time.

But something's not right. As if I don't already have enough crap swirling around in my head, now there's Doug Rhinebach. And while I believe Emily when she says that Aurora's been true to me, it was pretty obvious tonight that Aurora hasn't exactly been giving Doug the cold shoulder.

I should be pissed. I *am* pissed. But I'm also burdened by this tendency to see the other side of things.

Can I really blame her for hedging her bets? Isn't it human nature to try to protect yourself from being devastated? She knew there was a chance I wouldn't come back. That just adds to what I owe her for waiting for me.

She rests quietly in my arms. We listen to each other's breaths. We're parked in the woods at the end of a road marked private. No one knows why this road is here. Years ago Trey bought the yellow PRIVATE ROAD sign and hammered it onto a tree at the entrance. It's been our private road ever since.

It's quiet. Is Aurora thinking about Doug? Has she parked here with him?

Stop it, Jake. You know damn well she hasn't.

"Do you *have* to go back?" she asks.

"It's what I'm supposed to do."

She runs her finger along the cast. "After what you've been through, it doesn't seem right."

Tell me about it. And yet, there's always the other side of the story. "Suppose I sold cars for a living. And I have this fantastic day where I sell more cars than anyone's ever sold. And as I'm leaving the dealership, I trip on the curb and break my ankle. That mean I don't have to sell cars anymore?"

"Well, not if you sold a *million* cars that day." Aurora grins. And no, I don't think Doug's on her mind right now. She gently traces the scar on my chin with her fingers. "How long will you be away?"

If I go back? I just can't imagine doing that. Forget the medal. I'll return the enlistment bonus. I'll go to prison if they make me. Anything is better than being over there.

But I can't tell Aurora that. I can't burden her with a secret that momentous. My grandfather is one of the best-known generals alive. My father is a lieutenant colonel. This town loves its military and I am its hero. How can I embarrass my family and town? How can I thumb my nose at them?

I still haven't answered Aurora's question about how long I'll be over there if I finish my deployment. I have to make something up. "Six or seven months."

For a few moments she's still, and then she slides out of my arms and sits up. She looks out the window. I can't see her face. Somewhere in the dark distance a dog barks.

Without turning, Aurora asks, "Do you want me to wait for you?"

If ever there was a loaded question, this has to be it. Is she saying that she'd rather not wait? Is she saying she will only if I want her to? Or is she saying that she wants to wait, but feels like she needs more of a commitment? And what if I say yes, and then in a few days do what I know deep in my heart I should do? Then she'll get to be the girlfriend of "the former hero" who thumbed his nose at the military, who is suddenly the town pariah. Hell, a *national pariah*, as far as half this country thinks. It's a no-win situation for her.

ALJAHIM

I have to assume the sniper is coming down from the roof to finish me off. I get to my feet, M-16 aimed, swiveling, moving slowly along the side of a building. A dozen parts of my body throb and burn. Glancing back at the ground where I rolled to avoid being shot, there are splotches of red in the dirt.

The firefight is still going strong on the other side of the wall. Single shots and longer rips of full auto. Sounds like nonstop Fourth of July festivities. That's good news. There must be enough of our guys left from the convoy to give us a fighting chance of getting out of here.

But not without Skitballs. Is he still alive? He hasn't cried out for a minute or two.

And what about that damned sniper?

I slide along the wall to an open doorway and quickly glance in. Walled stairs go upward. I take them, expecting at any second to encounter the sniper coming down. But if

I can get to the roof, I can locate Skitballs.

A sound comes from above, from around the corner where the stairs double back. Just a soft thump. Is it the sniper? Is this a trap? Is he perched at the top of the next flight of stairs, waiting for me to come around the bend? I squat in the stairwell, aware of the heat, the pain in my legs, the dampness of my uniform where it's soaked with sweat and blood. There's no time to waste.

I toss a smoke grenade around the corner. Instantly there's rifle fire and rounds slam into the wall near me. I count three shots, then poke my M-16 around the corner and fire a couple of three-round bursts upward into the thick smoke. There's a grunt and a thud. Something metallic clatters down the steps. A second later a Russian-made Dragunov sniper rifle lies on the landing near me.

As soon as the smoke thins, I head up the stairs, stepping over the body of the dead sniper. At the top is a door, which I'm pretty sure leads to the roof. I kick it open and dive through in case there's another bad guy up there. But the roof is empty, save a couple of dozen shell casings from the Dragunov.

I'm back under the hot sun. The firefight is still going strong. Luckily, there are no roofs higher than this one, nowhere for a triggerman to fire down on me. Staying low, I creep toward the parapet, take off my helmet, and stick it on the muzzle of my M-16. When I hold it up to the edge of the parapet, no one shoots at it. I put the helmet back on and peek over the ledge.

On the road below is the line of damaged vehicles that was our convoy before the daisy-chained IEDs obliterated them. Every forty feet or so, there's a crater in the road. Some must be ten feet across and four feet deep. The IEDs were probably made from huge artillery shells. The sight of American bodies lying on the ground fills me with rage.

Below to my left, a bunch of our guys have formed a defensive position behind a couple of overturned vehicles. To my right, a soldier lies in what looks like an open sewer. From this distance, I can't be sure it's Skitballs, but if it is, that explains why the insurgents weren't able to finish him off. The sewer runs a foot or so below the level of the dirt road, keeping him out of their line of fire.

Farther down the road to my right, another group of our guys is hunkered down behind an overturned heavy tactical truck. When I check the roof above and behind them, I see someone wearing long, loose clothes and a cap. He's carrying an AK-47.

I aim and fire. The guy goes down. But how long before another takes his place? This firefight is turning into a real meat grinder. Meanwhile, the golden hour for Skitballs is fast ticking away. But as much as I need to get to him, I have to protect those guys on the road from another insurgent getting on that roof and firing down on them like fish in a barrel.

I climb over parapets until I'm right above them. From here I have a 180-degree view of the scene and can see what the soldiers below can't see—a pair of insurgents sneaking toward them along a wall. One has an AK, the other an RPG launcher.

Because they're to my right and down below hugging the wall, I'll have to lean out over the parapet and shoot lefty, not something I have a lot of experience doing. I set my weapon on three-round burst again, lean out, and try to take aim.

Thwuck! Next thing I know, I'm lying on my side halfway across the roof. My ears are ringing. While it doesn't seem possible, my heart feels like it's pumping even harder than before. I've been hit in the head, but I don't know by what. My hands go to my helmet. On one side is a hole where a bullet entered. Near the top of the helmet is a gash in the Kevlar where it exited.

The shot must've come from below. Had the bullet struck a half inch lower, it would have taken off the top of my skull. I still have to get those insurgents sneaking along the wall, but when I rise to my hands and knees, I suddenly feel light-headed. My peripheral vision starts to go gray and I think I'll either faint or puke.

Suck it up! I tell myself, lowering my head to the rooftop.

The sick feeling passes. I get into a crouch. Staying low, I cross the roof to a door, and down another set of stairs. Through a sun-washed courtyard to an arched doorway that opens to the street. Through the doorway, I should be able to see the guys pinned down behind the tactical truck. But instead, there's just empty road.

I've miscalculated.

DAD

Rap! Rap! Two short, quick knocks. I know who it is. "Come in, Dad."

My door opens and he strides in wearing his full lieutenant colonel's uniform with the tabs, badges, insignias, stripes, and bars—just about all the chest candy a soldier can earn without seeing action.

Lori's made some adjustments to my Class As, letting out the left pants leg so the cast will fit under it. As a private first class, I have a lot less egg salad on my chest than Dad does, but I do have one he'll never have—the Combat Action Badge.

It's hardly two inches long, a wreath with a bayonet and a grenade. Rarely has something so small meant so much in the lives of those who've earned it.

And in the lives of those who haven't. Dad could have seen action in the Gulf wars, but a trick knee kept him out of the fight. He also comes from a military family. His father, Herbert Liddell, was a Navy commander, and Dad's brother was a Navy fighter pilot. Both saw action in the Gulf War. Dad's always been a quiet, stoic sort of soldier. Maybe not as gung-ho as some others, but someone who accepted his lot and did his job.

Before I enlisted, I felt bad that he was the only one in our family who'd never been in battle. Now I can't help thinking how lucky he's been.

He's never had to kill another human being. The memory of the first time I did is still as vivid as it was the moment it happened. One moment there was the swarthy, bearded bad guy I'd been trained to kill. The next moment there was a fallen soldier who'd probably believed as firmly in his cause as I did in mine. I'd taken a life, done something that could never be undone. My father doesn't have to be haunted by that.

"Ready?" Dad asks. It's time for my next "engagement." Not with the enemy, but with a select group of the General's two hundred closest "friends."

"I guess." *Now appearing at the carnival sideshow. The bearded lady. The sword swallower. The wounded military hero.*

"We'll try to make it as painless as possible," Dad says with a thin smile.

He means it. And I appreciate that. Ever since I deployed, things have been a lot different between us. A lot better. Back in high school, you wouldn't believe the fights we had. For three years he was on my butt 24/7.

Why wasn't I getting better grades? Not that they were terrible. They just weren't great.

Why wasn't I captain of a team? It wasn't enough to be a starting second baseman or cornerback. I had to show leadership.

Why wasn't I volunteering or doing any extracurricular activities?

For him, it was all about me getting into Hudson High, the USMA, West Point. The first step toward becoming a high-ranking officer in the military. That's what he'd done. That's what I'd been told I would do since the moment I'd marched around the living room in a diaper with a plastic rifle on my shoulder.

It came to a head the day I enlisted. I didn't get home until early evening. Dad was in the backyard spreading manure in his vegetable garden. When he saw me, he stopped and leaned on the shovel. It had been a hot day and swallows were wheeling and diving in the air above us, snatching whatever flying insects had just hatched. Up close, the acrid smell of the compost manure burned my nostrils.

"I signed up," I said.

It didn't come as a surprise. I'd told him that was what I planned to do. He pursed his lips. Behind them, he was probably clenching his teeth. "Write a letter to the recruiting commander telling him you've changed your mind."

"I'm not doing that, Dad."

He just stared. There wasn't a lot about me enlisting

that we hadn't already said, shouted, screamed at each other a dozen times. He wanted me to go to West Point so that I wouldn't have to enter the Army as a grunt infantryman—the most likely to see action, the most likely to be killed or wounded.

I argued that neither his father nor the General had taken that route. Both had enlisted and seen action in Vietnam. His father had made it to Navy commander. The General was, of course, the General. I wanted to prove myself just as my grandfathers had. I didn't want to have life handed to me on a platter. I didn't want to go to West Point and have everyone think I was a shoo-in because of my famous family.

Overhead, the swallows rose and dove. I braced myself for Dad to start shouting. Or pull out his phone and call someone at recruiting headquarters. But he did neither. Instead, he stared at the ground and blinked hard. His eyes suddenly looked watery. It was probably the acrid stink of the manure that did it. "Go back in the house," he said, then turned away and started shoveling again.

Now, in my room, he steps close and tightens the knot of my tie, straightens my Combat Action Badge. He claps me on the shoulder and smiles. "See you downstairs, soldier." He does an about-face and heads back down.

My phone vibrates. *Aurora?* I wonder hopefully as I reach for it. We haven't spoken since I dropped her at her house last night. Actually, we haven't spoken since the moment she asked me if I wanted her to wait for me.

I can't help thinking about what happened to Skitballs. One night, probably about a month into our deployment, we were in the DFAC eating dinner and suddenly there was a loud *bang!* and food went flying. Everyone dove for the floor, thinking it was an incoming and we were under attack.

But we heard a *clang!* And someone cursing up a storm. And another *clang!* So it wasn't an attack. We got to our feet and there was Skitballs going nucking futs, ranting like a madman and smashing a metal tray against the edge of the table. Glasses fell over, spilling bug juice and milk. Sugar shakers rolled off the table and crashed to the floor.

Guys started yelling at him to stop because he was making a mess and ruining dinner, but Skitballs ignored them. Morpiss and I decided to take the calm approach and started toward him. Only when he saw us, he grabbed the napkin dispenser and reared back like he was going to throw a hundred-mile-per-hour fastball straight at our heads.

That's when Brad came out of nowhere and tackled him. He wrestled Skitballs to the floor and pinned him. Skitballs was still cursing. And now we knew it was about his girlfriend. The one whose credit card debt he'd paid off with his enlistment bonus.

Only it sounded like she wasn't his girlfriend anymore.

When Skitballs had calmed down, Morpiss and I took him back to the barracks. The poor guy had only been away from home for a month and his girlfriend had taken his money and dumped him.

"She said she'd wait!" Skitballs sobbed, wiping his eyes and nose on his sleeve. "She promised!"

In the barracks, he washed down a couple of pills because there was no hooch allowed. By now the anger had mostly passed and he was bawling. That was the thing about Skitballs. He wore his heart on his sleeve. If he could be that open and honest about his feelings, you knew you could trust him.

But even back then it seemed to me that anyone who was really going to wait for you didn't have to ask if you wanted them to.

In my room, a text comes up on my phone. But it's not Aurora. It's Brandi: **Meet again?**

THE GENERAL

The General's house has tall white columns in the front, verandas all around, and probably eight fireplaces. His idea of "a little get-together" is a catered affair in the backyard with a dozen tables covered with white tablecloths, crystal, china, and silver. A crowd of well-dressed people hoist drinks and stand around yakking. I chat with the mayor of Franklin, a US congressman, and a couple of state senators, as well as an assortment of military brass and well-to-do business folk.

In the lull that follows the usual hero questions, I feel a hand close on my elbow and tug. It's Lori. She stretches up on her toes and whispers into my ear, "Come with me."

"He's milking your medal for all it's worth," my sister growls in a low voice once we're out of earshot of the crowd. "He only got the bronze. You're in line for the silver. Someone said the governor may even show up."

On the surface, this affair serves a number of purposes

for the General. It is the celebration of a local hero (who just happens to be his grandson). It's a demonstration of the pride our town takes in its military. It's a chance for the bigwigs to rub shoulders with a hero, and a chance for me to get on their radar, no matter what career I eventually choose. Military, business, politics. Take your pick.

But under the surface, there are some less obvious reasons for this shindig. First and foremost, to remind everyone that the General is still a force to be reckoned with . . . in this town, in this state, maybe even in this country. Second, it's an opportunity to make it clear to everyone that my "hero genes" come from his—my mother's—side of the family.

Because in the General's mind there's no possible way those genes could have come from the Liddell—my father's—side. Not with my desk jockey father and, even worse, the Liddells' dark, treasonous past.

Lori walks me toward the tables, spread out on the lawn. Most don't have place cards, but as we get closer to the portable podium, the cards start to appear. We arrive at the head table, where one chair is bracketed by an American flag on the left and the flag of the US Army on the right. The card on the plate says PFC Jake Liddell, yours truly.

We circle the table, checking out the other place cards. Some of the names I recognize, some I don't.

"Douglas Erwin? Pat Petersen?" I whisper to Lori.

"I think Petersen's the chairman of Precision General Corporation," she whispers back. "Big defense contractor. No idea who Erwin is."

I've always been aware that the General hobnobbed with corporate bigwigs. Back in high school, I didn't bother to pay attention to that kind of stuff. Who cared what company made the Humvees, troop carriers, body armor, and weapons? But then I got sent over there. When you're at war, the quality of your gear can be the difference between life and death. When Morpiss would ask me to help him weld extra iron plating—hillbilly armor, he called it—to the undercarriages of our vehicles, he'd give me an earful about how badly made some of our gear was.

"Never forget, my friend," he'd say. "Your life is in the hands of the lowest bidder."

I always thought it was interesting that Morpiss—pretty much a hillbilly himself, poor and from the sticks—knew more about the business of war than almost anyone else I met in the service.

Now, here at the General's shindig, something tells me that some of those lowest bidders will be seated at this table with the General and me. "Remind me what the General has to do with these guys?" I ask Lori.

"He sits on their corporate boards."

"And translated into English, that means?"

"It means . . . it's time to start drinking." Lori points at the bar and heads that way. I know my sister and her moods. Something's ticked her off big-time. Dad says she takes after Mom—born with a built-in BS detector. I have to crutch it double-time to catch up to her as she stomps away muttering, "I can't believe it. I just *can't* believe it."

"Can't believe what?" I ask.

"Did you see a place card for Dad? It's so obnoxious. Not just obnoxious but downright insulting."

I can't argue. The General has been subtly demeaning Dad for as long as I can remember. It's because of our "treasonous past." Because Dad had an uncle named David Liddell who brought shame to the Liddell side of the family. But in the coming days, if I do what I think I should do, the General may feel the need to distance himself from me as well. Only that will be a lot harder. He's an older man now. Near the end of his career, whether he admits it or not. He's never been anything but kind and loving to Lori and me. If I go through with my plan, he will be forced to live his final years in humiliation.

Can I really do that to him?

We arrive at the outdoor bar. Behind a row of glimmering stemware, the bartender looks familiar. His black ponytail is tucked under the collar of a white shirt. And that collar is pulled up high to cover as much of his thick, black neck tattoo as possible. It's Barry, the former bassist with Brad's band, the Zombie Horde.

We clasp hands and exchange greetings. It's good to see him.

"Still playing?" I ask.

"Here and there." The way Barry shrugs says he's not playing much. "You've sure made it big."

"Not quite the same way."

"Sure you could," Barry says. "We'll put together an

act called Jake Liddell and the War Heroes. I'll write the songs. Guaranteed a hundred thousand Spotify plays the first week."

Lori pokes me with her elbow. "Why not? It beats getting shot at."

"I'll think about it," I tell Barry, and we both know I won't. I just might be the most unmusical person who ever lived.

I introduce Barry to my sister, who orders a Long Island iced tea. I have a Patron on the rocks with a lime wedge. We may be underage, and the General may be a straight arrow, but the one exception is the rule of booze. Real men and women drink.

And learn how to hold their liquor at an early age.

Glasses in hand, we're about to rejoin the festivities when Barry asks in a low voice, "It true you and Brad were at the same base over there?"

I take a long, fortifying sip of Patron. Pretty sure I know what's coming next.

"And what I heard about Brad?" Barry says.

"He was a great squad leader and did everything he could to protect his men," I tell him. "I wouldn't be here right now if it wasn't for him."

"But I heard . . ." Barry lets the sentence trail off.

Yeah, he heard. But that is only one side of a complicated and tragic story. I'll defend Brad until the day I die. "Listen, man, no one who hasn't been over there has any idea."

Barry grimaces. "That bad?"

I take another sip of the Patron and feel the heat in my throat. I almost say, "Yeah, that bad," but something stops me. No complaints. No bellyaching. What's done is done. *Suck it up, soldier.*

Lori and I head back toward the tables. "Have you decided what you're going to do?" she asks quietly.

I shake my head. "I just don't know if I can."

As I crutch along, she rubs my back. "No matter what you decide, I'll support you. I'll always be proud of you, little brother."

She may be the only one.

Lori goes off to the table in Siberia where Dad has been banished, and I take my seat with the crème de la crème.

At the portable podium, the General tells the guests how proud he is of my heroism and contribution to the war effort. But it's not long before he's reminiscing about his own combat heroism in Vietnam. And from there it's all about his rise through the ranks while commanding troops in the Gulf wars, and finally being promoted to major general. Then, as if he knows he's spent too much time talking about himself, he winds up with a big rah-rah about the worldwide forces of evil seeking to destroy America, and how vital it is that we keep our military strong.

More speakers follow, all of them praising my heroism (and being sure to remind everyone of their long friendship with the General). Lori, sitting with Dad at that table near the back, looks like she's about to barf.

Finally, the affair ends, but we have to hang around until every guest has congratulated me one last time. Then, just when we're about to depart, the General takes me aside. "What are your plans, son?"

Even though he's my grandfather, it still feels a bit intimidating to be this close to an actual former major general who once commanded tens of thousands of troops. During my service so far, I haven't even *seen* the general who's in charge of my division.

The General's not asking about my plans for later tonight, or about the rest of my stay here before I allegedly head to Walter Reed for rehab. He's asking about the future. "I take it that none of your injuries are severe enough to prevent you from returning to active service?"

"That's my understanding, sir. Guess I was kind of lucky. The docs said if I'd lost any more of my ring finger, they'd have shoehorned me into an honorable discharge."

The General glances at his gold wristwatch. Then back at me. "We need to talk, son. Not now, but soon. Before I go out of town on business later this week."

He turns away. Guess it doesn't matter what I *think* my plans are. He's already decided for me.

BRAD

At FOB Choke Point, Brad's office was in a Conex box he shared with another squad leader. The door was slightly ajar. Not enough so that I could see in. I knocked. There was no answer. I knocked again.

Still no answer.

I nudged the door open just enough to peek. The office was paneled in raw plywood. Brad was sitting at his desk, hunched forward with his face in his hands. On the wall above his desk was a map of the valley.

"Private First Class Jake Liddell reporting." I thought he'd react when he heard my voice, but he didn't move.

"Uh, Staff Sergeant Burrows?" I said a little louder.

Nothing. If it wasn't for his slowly expanding and contracting chest, you wouldn't even know he was breathing.

I took a step closer. "You asked to see me, Staff Sergeant?"

"You really never touched her?" His voice was muffled by his hands. The question came from so far out of left field that for a moment I had no idea what he was talking about.

"Sorry? Oh, you mean . . . No, Staff Sergeant. Like I told you, we were just friends after that."

Brad raised his head just enough to look at me with reddened eyes. "But you *wanted* to, right?"

"No, I . . . It's hard to explain, Staff Sergeant."

He was looking at me now and I could tell something wasn't right. It was the way his eyes couldn't stay focused. The way he'd blink rapidly a bunch of times and then just stare. "Give it a try, Private. And from now on, when it's just you and me, you can address me as Sarge."

"Well, Sarge, to be honest, I was pretty torn up at first. I mean, who wouldn't be? I used to think about messing with your Vette. Key it. Smash the windshield. Slash the tires. That kind of stuff."

He smirked. "So why didn't you?"

Scratching sounds were coming from under the Conex box. Probably rats. "Two reasons, Sarge. The first was that you would have known who did it. And the second, I guess I'm just not that kind of person."

Brad rested his face in his hands again. As if it weighed so much that his neck wasn't strong enough to hold it up. "That's what Erin Rose said. So you really were just friends?"

"Yes, Sarge. I guess because of all the time we'd spent together. We knew each other pretty well."

It got quiet. Brad stared up at the map on the wall. Pinned along the margins were half a dozen photos of

Erin Rose, some with their daughter, Amber. When he finally spoke again, it was barely above a whisper. "She said you were a standup guy. None of that kiss-and-tell stuff."

So he knew. I never told anyone, so she must've told him.

"You think she's been faithful to me?" he asked in a raw, pained tone. It had to be hard for him to ask me—a mere grunt and his wife's former boyfriend—such a personal question.

"Honestly, Sarge, I believe she has." I thought then he'd turn his head and look at me. Maybe act relieved. Maybe even thank me.

But he didn't. I waited until he spoke again: "Doesn't appear that anyone around here knows about your grandfather, does it?"

"No, Sarge. And I appreciate that, Sarge. I really do."

"You asked me to do you that favor, Private."

"Yes, Sarge, I did."

"Can I trust you, Private Liddell?"

"In what way, Sarge?"

"In all ways, Private. What did Erin Rose say about you?"

"Uh . . . that I'm a standup guy. None of that kiss-and-tell stuff."

Now he looked at me, his eyes still bloodshot. "You ever see your squad leader all broken up about whether his wife had been faithful to him?"

"No, Sarge, I can't recall that, ever."

"That's correct. Now get your punk private first class ass out of here."

I did as ordered.

LORI

"Jake! Wake up!"

I open my eyes. The light is on and I'm sitting up in bed. Lori's face is close to mine. Her forehead is bunched with concern. She's got one hand on each of my biceps, and somehow I know she's been shaking me. I'm breathing hard, my heart is racing, and my pajamas feel damp. There's that split-second fear that I've pissed myself in my sleep. But it's never urine. It's always sweat.

"Oh my God, are you okay?" Lori's eyes are wide. She's wearing the baggy T-shirt she sleeps in.

"Yeah." I start to breathe easier, but my heart is still beating at speed-metal tempo. I was dreaming I was back at the ambush. On the roof, while the firefight continued on the street below. I was on my back, eyes blinded by the glaring sunlight. I tried to roll over but couldn't. It felt like my body armor was bolted to the roof. A shadow moved over me—that insurgent wearing loose clothes and a cap. He was aiming his AK down at me, point-blank. My hands were sliding all over on the sandy rooftop as I desperately felt for a weapon or anything to protect myself with. But there was nothing. I was trapped on my back and he was closing in. The dark tunnel of the AK's barrel growing larger and larger.

"You were yelling so loud. I've never heard anything like it. I kept shaking you, but you wouldn't wake up." Lori gives me a penetrating look, asking with her eyes what could have possibly happened over there that would result in such a violent dream. Of course, I've never told her about the really bad stuff. To talk about it is to relive it. To relive it is to refeel it. And I never want to feel anything like it again.

With the corner of the T-shirt, she wipes some sweat off my forehead. We sit for a while in silence. Finally, she says, "I know you don't want to talk about it, but if you ever change your mind . . ."

"Thanks."

She kisses me on the forehead and gets up, switching off the light as she leaves. I lie in bed, staring up into the dark, my heart gradually decelerating. At FOB Choke Point they gave us pills for night terrors. When I got to Landstuhl in Germany, I tried to stop taking them, but my nightly yelling woke the other patients on the ward. So I started again. Here at home I thought maybe being in safe, familiar surroundings might make a difference. I haven't taken a pill for the past three days, and tonight's the first time I've had the terrors. So maybe I'm getting better. Maybe I'll be one of the lucky ones.

BRANDI

Thanks for coming," she says. It's early morning and we're at Starbucks. Last year there was one Starbucks in town. Now there are three, including this one, directly across from the high school.

"I don't have much time," I tell her.

"That's fine." She's bought me a venti coffee. At FOB Choke Point we were a twitchy bunch. We'd usually down about a quart of battery acid each morning before switching over to Rip It energy drink for the rest of the day.

She's gotten a green tea latte for herself.

"Looks like pea soup with a cream topping," I quip while she opens her laptop.

She makes a face. "Thanks. I'll enjoy thinking about that while I drink it."

She's quick and funny. I enjoy our repartee. We're huddled at a table in the back of the store. Meanwhile, a steady stream of kids with backpacks is waiting in a long line for their pre-academic caffeine rush.

She's cued up a video on the laptop, but before she starts it, she says, "Let me ask you something, Jake. Do you find it ironic that the United States passed something called the Child Soldiers Prevention Act to stop other countries from recruiting child soldiers? Meanwhile, we have the largest child soldier recruitment program in the world?"

"What?" *Is she crazy?*

"Sorry," she says. "Did I say child soldier recruitment program? I meant JROTC."

Oh. "Larger than China's?"

"Okay, largest in the Western world."

JROTC starts in ninth grade, so kids begin to get "indoctrinated" at fourteen years old. Child recruitment indeed. But why is she telling me this? I glance at my watch. In a few minutes, Lori is going to swing by and take me to the bus station. In the meantime, shouldn't I be looking for Aurora? To try to figure out a way to fix things between us? And what about Erin Rose? I promised myself I'd find her. It's important. Way more important than sitting here discussing the evils of JROTC.

But something keeps me. Maybe it's the admiration I'm beginning to feel for Brandi, someone who thinks about more than herself. Someone who appears *willing to act* for a cause she believes in.

Brandi starts the video. It's the Franklin High School JROTC drill team in the gym before a crowd. The team is in full dress uniform, red berets, white ascots and gloves, aiguillettes. Following orders with precision, they smack their rifles in unison, slap the bolts open and slam them shut. Snap to attention. About-face and march. The drill master's barking orders fade, replaced by Brandi's voice-over: "According to the United States military, the Junior Reserve Officer Training Corps program is *not* a military preparation class. Meanwhile, the word 'training' appears constantly. Not just in the name of the program, but in its promotional literature as well. And like aspiring soldiers, members of JROTC are called cadets, wear uniforms, and have ranks. The instruction they receive mirrors military training in nearly every way. But let me repeat, the military says JROTC is *not* for the purposes of preparation in the military.

"You might also be interested to learn that the drill rifles and sabers that cadets train with are not to be considered weapons. They may look exactly like weapons, but the military says that is not what they are meant to be.

"If you find these statements puzzling, you are not alone. Just because the military *says* JROTC isn't a military preparation class doesn't mean it's true. Just because they *say* a drill rifle is not meant to represent a weapon doesn't mean it's true. They also claim they don't have weapons training, but the National Rifle Association contributes to JROTC. In return, JROTC encourages cadets to join the NRA and participate in marksmanship matches.

"If JROTC isn't a military preparation class, then why do roughly forty percent of its graduates go directly into the military? Meanwhile, less than two percent of all high school students nationwide go directly into the military.

"In other words, graduates from JROTC are twenty times more likely to enter the military than students who were not in JROTC. But, as I've said, the military still insists that the JROTC program is *not* military preparation."

The video ends. I feel Brandi's eyes. She's waiting for my response.

"I could argue with a few of your points," I tell her. "Drill rifles are just toys. But I get the idea."

"That's just the introduction," she tells me. "From there I want to point out that twelve percent of the American population is black, while thirty percent of the United States Army is black. Fifty percent of the enrollees in JROTC are black or minority. Wouldn't you say that sounds a little disproportionate?"

"But that's because the military offers opportunities for advancement," I suggest.

"You mean, for those who manage to survive whatever war we're currently involved in?" she asks. "And even if they do survive, fifty percent of homeless veterans are black. That doesn't sound like an opportunity for advancement to me."

"Look, it's an all-volunteer army," I counter. "It's not like anyone's being forced to sign up."

Brandi drills me with those hazel eyes. "Don't play dumb white cracker with me, Jake Liddell. Minorities in this country don't have anything close to the educational

85

or job opportunities that white people have. For a lot of minorities, the military is one of three options. The other two being an unlivable minimum wage, or crime and incarceration. Look at it that way and the military becomes the *only* option. Even if it means a serious risk to life and limb."

Okay, so it's obvious she's done her homework. This is important to her. And I guess what she's saying is true. But . . .

"Why tell me?" I ask.

It must be getting close to first bell. The line of students at the baristas has grown shorter. Brandi leans close. Her sweet fragrance strangely at odds with the flashing intensity in those eyes. "Because *you* could make a huge difference, Jake. You could speak out. Expose JROTC for the minority child military indoctrination program that it really is. You're a hero, the grandson of General Windy Granger. If you speak out, people will listen."

Okay, now I get it. But I'm curious. "Speak out how?"

Brandi's hazel eyes dart at the laptop screen.

"You want *me* to be in that video?" I realize.

"Yes." She tells me about the National Network Opposing the Militarization of Youth, Veterans for Peace, the War Resisters League, and the Project on Youth and Non-Military Opportunities. All organizations that actively oppose JROTC.

"I'll be honest with you, Jake," she says. "What you saw on my video is nothing new. But if I have you talk about your experience . . . *that* would make a huge impact. Then this video will become something that can really make a difference."

American War Hero Speaks Out Against JROTC. Calls It Minority Child Military Indoctrination.

I cross my arms and lean back. "I admire your determination, Brandi, but all the reasons that you just gave for why I should speak out are exactly the reasons why I can't. Because they say I'm a hero. Because I'm the grandson of Windy Granger. Because I went through JROTC myself. I'm not saying you're wrong. I agree that JROTC deserves an honest appraisal. And so does the Army itself. I'm just saying that were I to do that, it would be a betrayal verging on treason."

And not the first time the Liddell name and that word have been linked.

Brandi screws up her face. "How could it be treason? You're a—"

I hold up my hand. I've heard the h-word enough, and that's not the point. "There are thousands of minorities and whites who've gone through JROTC and are glad they did. Some went into the military, but a lot didn't. Look at it this way. JROTC gives students a taste of the military without them having to commit to it for two years. You can't say that's a bad thing."

Brandi scowls and pulls her lips in, but doesn't argue.

"And there's another reason," I continue. "I can't do it to my family. And I can't do it to the families of all the soldiers who went through JROTC and into the military and never came home. You've got one side of the story, Brandi. And you're right. It's definitely a side more people should know about. But it's not the only side."

Out of the corner of my eye, I see Lori's Honda pull up outside. I grab my crutches and start to get up. Brandi looks startled.

"Good luck with your video," I tell her. "And thanks for the coffee."

ALJAHIM

The two insurgents, one with an AK, the other with an RPG launcher, are still creeping along the wall toward the guys dug in behind the tactical truck. I was going to try to pick them off from the roof, but at the parapet I nearly got my head blown off when that bullet ripped through the top of my helmet. Meanwhile, the firefight continues. Hundreds of rounds a minute snapping, popping, exploding. It's mayhem.

I double back through the courtyard and into an alley, knowing each time I turn a corner I could run into someone who wants me dead. I'm passing a door when I hear something that makes me stop.

Pop! Pop! Someone on the other side of the door is shooting. And it's a pretty safe bet that if they're shooting from indoors, they're not on our side. I need to get to Skitballs. I need to warn the guys hunkered down behind the truck about the approaching insurgents. But I have to take care of this too.

I smash shoulder-first through the door. Inside, a woman screams. The room is dim. In the shadows I can barely make out two women in black abayas, one older and one younger, and a baby. Across the room is another doorway through which I can see daylight and the shooter kneeling at the window, his weapon resting on the sill.

I barrel through and get to him before he can turn around. It's a scrawny kid. Can't be more than twelve. He's got an ancient bolt-action rifle that looks like it could be a hundred years old. It's so long and heavy, the kid can barely lift it. I grab it by the fore stock and rip it out of his hands.

The kid cowers. Now what do I do? He's been shooting at Americans. For all I know, he may have wounded or even killed someone. Strangely, he's not looking at me. Instead, he's staring across the room. I spin, expecting to find another attacker. But it's a man, lying near the wall. His stubbled face is pale and sweaty, his shirt completely soaked with blood. He's glassy-eyed, his breaths fast and shallow.

He's dying.

And I'll bet every penny I have he's this kid's father.

Guess that explains why the kid was shooting at us.

I grab the kid by the arm and drag him into the other room, sit him down beside the old lady in the abaya, and stab a finger at him. The universal sign to stay put. Then I go back into the room with the dying man and close the door behind me.

I go to the window the kid was shooting through and look out just in time to see the two insurgents who are sneaking up on the men behind the truck. They've split up and are about to pounce.

"Hey, douchebags!" I shout.

Both spin. I plug the one closest to me, but the other has time to get off two shots. The next thing I know, I'm hurtling backward. The SOB got me.

An instant later, he's mowed down in a hail of fire from the guys behind the truck. Just as I'd hoped, they were alerted by my shout.

Outside, the firefight continues. In the room where the kid was shooting, I manage to sit up, my back against the wall. The spot in my side where I was hit feels like it's on fire. The wound is between my hip and rib cage. If I'm lucky, it's far enough to the right that it didn't puncture my colon. But I can't move without feeling a bolt of agonizing pain.

I'm only a couple of feet from the kid's dying father. He's still breathing rapidly, skin going gray, bleeding out. He's looking at me with a sad, bewildered expression. Just a little while ago we were trying to kill each other. Now we're sitting together, both wounded. One of us, if not both, is soon to meet his maker.

Would someone please remind me what the purpose of war is?

Two of the guys from behind the tactical truck come through the window. They freeze when they see my mortally wounded comrade, but I shake my head as if to say he won't be a problem. Meanwhile, I'm lucky because one of the guys is a medic. He shoots me full of morphine and dresses my wound with QuikClot, bandage, and tape.

The bleeding's under control. Loaded with painkiller, I stagger to my feet. The guys help me through the window and behind the overturned truck. The firefight's still pretty kinetic. A corporal thanks me for saving them from the AK and RPG guys. He tells me to stay low. They've called in air support. It won't be long now. I point at Skitballs, still lying in that open sewer in the middle of the road. "That's my buddy."

"Can't help him until we get support," the corporal says. Rifle and automatic fire are still snapping and cracking around us.

But there can't be much left of Skitballs's golden hour. And here's a medic who could mean the difference between life and death. "I have to get him."

"You'll never make it, Private," the corporal says. "From here to there is a wide-open shooting gallery."

"Cover me."

If you're wondering why the corporal doesn't argue, I think it's because he wants to believe that if he was the guy lying in that open sewer, someone would come for him. I start to crawl out from behind the overturned truck. The dirt road around me begins to explode with rounds slapping into the ground. The guys behind the truck are laying down all the suppressive fire they can.

I get to Skitballs. His anxious eyes are open, a little glassy. A bubble of blood slowly forms in one nostril, then pops. He's lying in this open sewer, enveloped in the stink of human waste, the muck around him reddened by his blood.

I'm almost positive he's been hit in more than one place, but most of the bleeding's coming from his right thigh. There's a good chance the femoral artery's been severed. If Skitballs is going to live, I've got to stop the bleeding.

I reach for my IFAK, but it's not there. No idea where I lost it, but it's not like I'm gonna crawl back behind the tactical truck and borrow someone else's first aid kit. The only thing I can think of using as a tourniquet is the ripcord that holds my body armor in place.

It's pandemonium around us. The air is crackling with fire. Clots of dirt kick up. I use the knife on my Leatherman to cut the ripcord and tie it around Skitballs's thigh above the wound. Then I grab him by the shoulders. "Hold on, man, we're going home."

It was while dragging him back to the truck that I took the rounds to my left leg, the ones that broke my femur and ankle and hand.

Next thing I remember, I was in a chopper. Someone near me was screaming in pain.

A couple of days later I found out that Skitballs didn't make it. Neither did Clay, whose Army career ended the moment the daisy chain of IEDs went off. And Magnet?

Knocked out cold by the initial blast. Unconscious for the entire firefight. Later found unharmed under our overturned Humvee.

Some guys really do have all the luck.

MORPISS

Y'all sure you want to do this?" Morpiss's mother said on the phone.

"Doesn't he want me to?" I asked.

"Oh honey, does he. Just makin' sure y'all's prepared."

I guess that meant I wasn't. But I was going, no matter what.

That was a few weeks ago, while I was still being paraded around by the Army PR machine. I'd already told Aurora that when I got home, one of the things I had to do was go see Morpiss (I didn't tell her that another person I had to see was Erin Rose). Aurora had asked if she could drive me, and I was sorely tempted to accept the offer. It's a six-hour bus ride into another state. Six hours on a bus with my leg in a cast. I wasn't sure how that was going to work. But I didn't want her to go. It wasn't that I didn't want her to see Morpiss. The truth is, I didn't want Morpiss to see *her*. I didn't want to be the one who showed him what he might never have again.

Anyway, Aurora driving me is no longer an issue. We still haven't spoken since the other night in the car. I miss her badly. I'm only supposed to be here a few more days before I go to Walter Reed for PT. Whether or not that actually happens, it's crazy that I've finally come home and now we're not talking. But Aurora asked if I wanted her to wait. I feel like I have to give her an out. If I do what I hope I'll have the guts to do, the Army won't be sending me to Walter Reed. They won't be sending me anywhere, and I'll be in Franklin for the foreseeable future (unless the local folk run me out of town). And under those circumstances, I'm not sure Aurora will want much to do with me.

The bus driver suggests I sit in the way back, where people won't have to step over or go around my cast. So that's where I am, with the toilet smells and the diesel fumes seeping in. The heat from the engine creeps up through the seat, making my butt itchy. Want to know what it's like in the war zone? Try sitting in the back of a bus. Not for six hours. For six months.

Over there, the stink of the crappers, the diesel fumes from the generators, and the itchy heat rash were constants. So was the daily nerve-rattling barrage of rockets. Still, we were curious about what it was like outside the wire. At first, we only went on short patrols, never far enough to come face to face with the enemy. Sometimes at night we'd hear distant small arms fire. But it was faint and far away.

Then one morning at the daily briefing we heard that in a town about ten miles to our south some local kids had tripped a land mine while playing outside. A couple of them were killed. High command wanted the mines cleared out. This gesture was supposed to show the local populace who their *real* friends were. *Yeah, right.* US soldiers come from five thousand miles away, don't speak a word of their language, and terrorize their people with our killer drones. *Real friends for sure.*

We got the order to be ready to push out at ten hundred hours. This would be our first real foray into enemy territory. In the barracks, some guys were quiet. Others chattered nervously.

"Could be the real deal," Skitballs said while he strapped on his armor. "Romeo Squad's first engagement."

"Man, every time y'all set foot outside the wire, you're in enemy territory," Morpiss said.

"But this time we're pushin' deep," said Skitballs. "Just hope we're in the MRAP."

MRAP stood for mine-resistant ambush-protected vehicle. Usually truck-sized with enough Frag Kit 6 armor plating to stop just about any projectile, and a V-shaped undercarriage to deflect the explosive force of land mines.

"We should all be in MRAPs," muttered a new guy named Clay Gomez. He was stocky, muscular, tattooed, very serious. On Clay's first day at FOB Choke Point, Magnet had suggested "Taco" for his nickname because he was Hispanic. It took three of us to pull Clay off him.

After that, he was just Clay. Proud, tough, and not one to mess with.

"Ain't happening, man," said Morpiss. "They only got one MRAP to spare. And y'all can bet the sappers'll be in it."

"Sappers?" said Magnet.

"The EOD guys. Explosive Ordnance Disposal techs."

"What about M dogs?" suggested Clay.

"Negative," said Morpiss. "I heard the CO say command ain't got no teams to spare."

"It true in the Humvee you should always put your feet one in front of the other?" asked Magnet.

"What're you talkin' about, man?" Skitballs asked.

"If an IED goes off, there's more of a chance you'll keep one foot than if they're side by side."

Skitballs laughed. "Magnet, you are one crazy wombat." But military life was filled with nutty superstitions like that. Washing your patrol cap, eating the green Charms candy, saying the word "rain" while out on patrol. That was all bad juju. It might seem silly until you remembered that you were in an environment where death could sweep in at any moment without reason or warning. Given that, there was no limit to the lengths a guy would go to try to stay alive.

A few minutes before ten, all geared up, we headed out into the sunlight. The MRAP and Humvees were lined up, ready to go. Since we were being platooned, Lt. Abrams was the commanding officer. Standing in the sunlight, with Brad beside him, the lieutenant told us the EOD squad would ride with him in the MRAP. Romeo Squad, now under the immediate command of Sgt. Burrows, would ride in Humvees.

In other words, Brad would be my direct commander.

Morpiss, being a gearhead, always wanted to drive. Brad took the front passenger seat. I got in behind Morpiss, and Skitballs got in behind Brad. Clay manned the M-2 Browning in the gun turret.

"Commissioned officers ever ride in Humvees, Staff Sergeant Burrows?" Skitballs asked while he nervously readjusted his body armor.

"Not if they can avoid it, Private," Brad said.

"Wouldn't it set a good example, Staff Sergeant?"

"Of rank stupidity," Brad grunted.

"Lt. Abrams has earned it," Morpiss said. "Perks of the job. Longer you're in the military, the more experience y'all have. The more experience, the more valuable y'all are. So they got more reason to keep y'all alive."

"So . . . we're not valuable?" Skitballs asked.

No one answered.

With the MRAP in the lead, we left FOB Choke Point and headed down the bumpy dirt road, leaving a long plume of yellow dust behind. Ahead of us, the MRAP accelerated.

"Why the rush, Staff Sergeant?" Skitballs said.

"We push in and out fast," Brad said. "The less time the locals have to spread the word we're there, the better."

The Humvee went over a bump. In the backseat, Skitballs's and my helmets banged against the roof.

Everyone was pensive, quiet. We watched the landscape roll past. Flatlands with some greenery and a tree here and there. Busted old tanks and artillery from bygone wars. Tall weeds growing up through the rusted skeletons of trucks. Bomb craters so old that full-grown trees rose out of them. It felt like the land had been at war since the beginning of time.

After a while, a village appeared in the distance to our left. To our right rose a valley terrace. "That's our destination," said Brad.

"If this is hostile territory, won't we be sittin' ducks up there, Staff Sergeant?" asked Morpiss nervously.

"Affirmative, soldier. That's why we're moving, as the poet says, fleet afoot. Hopefully, if there are any bad guys around, they haven't had time to prepare."

The valley terrace looked like a small butte. It was grassy, treeless, covered here and there with small boulders and bare patches of dirt. It sloped up twenty or thirty yards from the road and then went kind of flat. Our small convoy came to a stop beside it. We had no way of knowing if there were any insurgents in the area, so Brad posted lookouts.

The engineers fanned out with PSS 14 mine detectors. They called them "pissers." Usually, when it came to mines, the sappers would use HRI mine rollers, basically remote control vehicles built to withstand being "blowed up." But the terrain was filled with small ravines and gullies that an HRI couldn't maneuver in. So the sappers had to cover it by foot.

They started sweeping and we followed, watching for any bad guys, slowly working our way up the gullies and ravines toward the top. The engineers didn't go fast. They didn't want to miss a single spot where a local kid could . . . *BOOM!*

We all flinched, then looked around. A ball of black smoke rose from the next gulley over.

"*Ahh! Ahh! Ahh!*" came the screams. We couldn't see who it was. At first, I thought it must have been one of the engineers. "*Ahhh! Ahhh!*" But it was Morpiss. I knew his voice. "*Oh God! Oh Mother! Help me! Help me!*"

A confusion of shouts followed: "Casualties!" "Everyone okay?" "Who's good?" "Tourniquet!"

"*Ahhh! Ahhh!*" Morpiss's anguished cries were like shock waves. They blew through you, tearing you up inside. We still couldn't see him. He must have fallen into some kind of depression.

"We're coming!" someone shouted.

"Morphine!" someone else shouted.

"We got you, man!"

"*Romeo, do not move!*" Brad's booming order rose above the other voices. "You hear me, Romeo? *Do . . . Not . . . Move!*"

"*Ahhh! Ahhh!*" I'd heard guys in pain before. A broken arm in football. An ankle snapped in a bad slide into second base. But I'd never heard a sound like that. Pure sonic agony. You couldn't listen without feeling sick.

"He'll need a tourniquet!" shouted someone who

wasn't near enough to see Morpiss. *They already knew. You stepped on a land mine....*

"Do . . . Not . . . Move!" Brad shouted again. "Could be plastic mines. That's why the sappers missed them."

Plastic land mines are almost impossible to detect without an HRI. The engineer's pissers were probably useless from the start. It had just been a matter of time until someone stepped on one.

"*Ahhh! Ahhh! It hurts!*" The agony in Morpiss's voice was so plaintive and raw it made me want to puke.

"We got you, man! We're coming!" Magnet shouted.

But no one moved. We were frozen. Hearts pounding so hard you half expected blood to burst out of your ears.

The platoon medic, following a sapper with ground-penetrating radar, finally reached Morpiss. "Need another tourniquet!"

"You know what that means," Skitballs muttered near me.

"*Ahhh! Ahhh! It hurts!*" Morpiss's screams pierced like hot, rusty needles.

"Get another tourniquet out!" That would be the third.

Brad ordered the rest of us back down the hill. "Only step in footprints someone else has made! Let's go! Let's go!"

He was rushing us. Any locals who'd heard the blast would know that we were there. Humping down from the rise, we were exposed and easy targets. A triggerman's dream.

But I wondered if there wasn't another reason Brad

wanted to get us off the terrace. The medic had called for three tourniquets. You only needed one per limb. Was Brad moving us out because he didn't want us to see what that meant?

We gathered around the vehicles. Morpiss wasn't screaming anymore. They must have had a morphine drip going. Someone put a purple smoke out for the dust-off.

We weren't going anywhere until the medevac chopper arrived. We had to provide cover in case a bad guy took a shot at it. For the first time since I'd arrived at FOB Choke Point, I half wished someone *would* take a shot. I was filled with fury and despair. Morpiss and Skitballs were the first friends I'd made on active duty. They were both honest, up-front guys. Never shirked their duties or tried to find an easy way out. The three of us had arrived at FOB Choke Point in the same chopper and had been assigned to the same squad. From day one we'd been best buds and rarely out of each other's sight.

Only now Morpiss was severely WIA. For his sake, I wanted to fight, kill. Beat the enemy bloody with my bare hands. Those bastards had just blowed up my buddy and I wanted to make them pay.

"Dabble Corners!" the bus driver calls out.

I open my eyes and look out the window. There's no town. Just a crossroads with a general store, a church, and a bar. Waiting in a banged-up old pickup truck is a woman with long gray hair and tired eyes. She looks about twenty years too old to be Morpiss's mom.

"I didn't know y'all was hurt," she says after I clamber into the truck.

"I'm on the mend, ma'am."

"Happened over there?"

"Yes, ma'am."

"James is mighty excited to see you. He don't hear much from the others."

It appears that Morpiss hasn't told his mom why that might be the case.

Soon we're on a narrow paved road, passing farms and houses with livestock wandering in the yards. Here and there is a lawn covered with scattered farm equipment, old furniture, or abandoned cars. Scrawny dogs chained to stakes. Chickens pecking around. Real rural America.

Some guys enlisted because they felt it was their duty. Some because it was the only paying job they could find. For Morpiss it was all those things. Plus it was probably the only chance he had of getting out of the sticks.

"Y'all ready to do some fishin'?" Mrs. Morris asks in the truck.

I give her a puzzled look. We've left the pavement and are bouncing down a backwoods dirt road. It's hard to understand why anyone would want to live this far away from everything. Just before I got into the pickup, I checked my cell phone. No bars.

"You'll see," she says. "He's got himself a setup. Just don't let him smoke the whole time, okay?"

So she knows. Guess I shouldn't be surprised.

The dirt road is no longer a road, just a long, long driveway. We come to a clearing where a small rickety house sits. The outside walls are patched where the siding has been replaced. The roof shingles are different colors where leaks have been patched. A wooden ramp leads up to the front door. The entire house could fit in the General's living room.

"Y'all ready?" Mrs. Morris asks.

I nod, even though I have a feeling I'm not.

"He's real happy to see you, but it ain't good."

"I understand, ma'am."

She gives me a sideways look as if asking, *"Can you really?"*

A big light-brown dog bounds toward me. I just have time to brace myself before his paws are on my shoulders and he's licking my face.

"Git down, Bandit!" Morpiss follows. He's belted into a wheelchair that he steers by joystick with his right hand.

Don't stare, I tell myself. *Do Not Stare.*

The lower half of his body is gone. Not just his legs, but the bottom part of his abdomen. Morpiss got his nickname because he had a bladder like a camel. He could drink for hours without going, but when he went, it sounded like Niagara Falls. He probably hit the pisser once a day, and you could get in a short nap before he came out. Now I'm not even sure he *has* a bladder.

We clasp hands. "Yo, hero boy, glad you came," he says. "Hope y'all don't mind if I'm only half the man I used to be."

"How many times have you used that line?" I ask.

"Not that much. Don't get a lot of visitors out this way." He rubs Bandit's head and nods at my cast. "Don't think I read about that. How'd that happen?"

"Skiing accident."

"Yeah, I hear them enemy black diamonds are a real bitch." He grins.

After the long bus ride, I need to go myself. The bathroom shelves are filled with powders, salves, various skin-colored patches, and curled lengths of clear and brown tubing. A jar of lubricant. An enema bag. *Oh jeez.* With only one arm he probably can't do that himself.

Who takes care of him? Is it just his mom 24/7?

Mrs. Morris serves us lunch. Fried bologna sandwiches, cold macaroni salad, glasses of Mountain Dew. Morpiss eats with his one hand. His left arm was severed by the blast. Both legs blown off at the knees. So why the extreme amputations? Because the explosion shattered both femurs, and the blast drove dirt and debris into his lower body, resulting in infections so severe that the tissue couldn't be saved.

Truth is, it's a miracle he's alive.

"Let's go fishin'," he says as soon as lunch ends.

Morpiss has rigged a rod carrier to the back of his wheelchair. Followed by Bandit, we go out the back door. The scent of burning wood is in the air. A long ramp behind the house leads to a small lake. At the end of the ramp is a platform with a low rail around it. I guess so Morpiss won't accidentally get pulled off the edge while fighting Moby Dick.

"Who built this?" I ask.

"Folks around here. They know I like to fish."

He's wearing a strap-on fishing rod holder that allows him to cast with one arm. He's even got a small spring-action vise that steadies the hook while he baits it with a minnow. Morpiss the geardo, always a resourceful guy. At FOB Choke Point he made us small fans from ice cream sticks, tape, soda bottles, and little electric motors that ran off the USB ports in our laptops.

"Go on, set yerself up." He points at another rod. "Don't expect me to do it just because y'all broke your leg."

Even now he can joke. I bait a hook, cast it out, and ease myself into a rusty lawn chair. Bandit settles down beside the wheelchair. The wooden rail is covered with short dark cigarette burns. "People come out and fish with you?"

"When they want to learn from the master. So, y'all bring what I asked for?"

I wedge the butt of the fishing rod under my leg and take out a brand-new vape pen. Morpiss's smile grows wide. "You are the man, PFC Jake Liddell."

"I don't remember you smoking at Choke Point."

"Never did. It's a dirty, disgusting habit that'll take years off your life."

"So why'd you start?" I ask without thinking.

Morpiss smirks. "You're kiddin', right?"

Like it's really going to make a difference now if he lives a few extra years or not. . . .

Morpiss takes a deep drag and lets out a big satisfied white plume. "Oh man, life just got good!"

And there we are. The triple amputee and the hero. Our situations could have so easily been switched. I could have stepped on that mine. He could have been the hero. Go ahead and tell me there's a reason things happen the way they do.

Just don't ask me to believe it.

The red-and-white bobber on Morpiss's line disappears under the surface. The tip of his fishing rod jiggles. There's a fish on, but Morpiss doesn't reel.

"You gonna bring that monster in?" I ask.

"Naw. It's small fry. Ain't a fish in this lake I ain't caught five times. If I let it run around, maybe somethin' bigger'll come along and eat it."

"That really happens?"

"Once in a while."

The conversation shifts to the war and our buddies. Magnet is always a good topic for all the times he nearly got hit and walked away unscratched. Talking about the other guys isn't much fun.

"Made many new pals?" Morpiss asks.

"Didn't want to." No matter what the recruiters want you to believe, the Army is never ever going to be a big frat party. You go in, make a couple of friends, and then pray you'll all make it out alive. All you have to lose is one buddy to discover the last thing you want to do is replace him with someone new. No point in getting close to anyone else you might lose the next day.

"How's it feel to be a hero?" Morpiss asks.

"About what you'd expect."

"A lot of beautiful young honeys throwin' themselves at you?"

"Only in the movies."

An osprey sweeps low over the lake, then banks upward and settles on a tree branch. Morpiss once told me he was a virgin when he enlisted. And now? Obviously, he's missing the essential equipment. Why? Because some higher-up thought it would be good PR if we cleared out some mines where kids wanted to play. The same kids who in a few years will be taught how to kill coalition troops.

The voice in my head says, *Let it go, Jake.*

Bandit yawns and rolls over. I didn't come just to see Morpiss. I came to talk. If there's one soldier in this world I can share my thoughts with, it's him. "I feel like we got railroaded, man. From the moment we started playing *Call of Duty.* And saw those Army ads about honor and leadership. Army Strong, right? The Army'll make you stronger, wiser, and more respected. Not a word about how it can also make you more wounded and more dead. Cigarette ads have health warnings. Every bottle of booze has a health warning. Everyone's freaked out about football players getting TBI. What about all the soldiers with TBI? How come they never put health warnings on Army recruitment ads? Warning: Enlistment in the United States Army may lead to traumatic and post-traumatic stress, brain injury, inability to function in normal society, loss of limbs, loss of life, suicide."

The little fish on Morpiss's line is zigging and zagging frantically, doing everything it can to shake the hook. Meanwhile, any second now something bigger may come along and devour it.

"Someone's got to take it to the enemy," Morpiss says.

"I know. I just think these kids who enlist should be given a better idea of what they're in for."

"Do that and no one'll enlist. The bad guys'll love you for it."

This is where the argument always ends. We *have* to fight because they *want* to fight. Even if it's true that sometimes the reason they want to fight is because we're the big bad USA claiming there are WMDs here and terrorists there. But what does that matter to grunts like Morpiss and me?

That little fish, still struggling for its life, is getting on my nerves. "Could you do something about that? It's starting to bug me."

Morpiss reels the little guy in. It's a bluegill, maybe four inches long. With a jerk of his arm, Morpiss deftly unhooks the fish and sends it splashing back to freedom.

My friend savors another hit of vape. "Ever consider

the idea that what you're feelin' could be natural given what y'all have been through?"

He's asking *me*? If anyone should feel angry and resentful about what they've been through . . .

"I think I'm seeing it pretty clearly," I tell him.

He baits his hook again, casts it back out. Ripples spread when the bobber splashes into the surface, but then the lake goes glassy flat again. Birds call and frogs croak. A dragonfly zips past and then hovers over a lily pad. There's peace here. I'm starting to get a sense of why some people would want to be this far away.

"Still got about half a year on your deployment, right?" Morpiss says as if he can feel where our conversation might be going.

"Maybe."

There it is. First time I've said it out loud to anyone other than Lori.

He gives me a sidelong glance. "Serious? Even with a big ol' medal comin' your way?"

The degree of my seriousness comes and goes. But when it goes, I suspect it's because I'm feeling scared. Scared to take a stand and do what deep down in my heart I believe is right. Scared of the disgrace it'll bring to the General. The liberal media would have a field day with it. No doubt they'd dig up the fact that Dad's uncle David was a Vietnam War draft dodger. And now there'd be me, the war hero who refused his medal, who refused to return to active duty, who told anyone who'd listen that war is immoral. That it is nothing more than mass murder. That enlistment bonuses make us hired killers. That any politician who thinks American troops should be sent to war must be forced to make his or her own children lead the fight.

Then we'll see how many politicians want their country to go to war.

"What if I was serious?" I ask.

A pair of mallards glides overhead and lands on the water.

"Your family . . . ," Morpiss begins, then goes quiet. On the lake, the mallards do that thing where their heads go down and their feathery butts point up in the air.

So he knows about my family.

Morpiss must feel the need to explain because he adds, "Y'all can't open a book about Iraq without readin' about General Windy Granger. He's right there in Wikipedia, too."

"But my last name's Liddell," I remind him.

"Google Liddell in Franklin and a Lieutenant Colonel Richard A. Liddell comes up. Follow it back a few pages and y'all get to a weddin' announcement between him and a Miss Sutton S. Granger, daughter of old Windborne himself. Man, if I had that kind of brass hat in my family . . ." He trails off.

My bobber goes under and I reel in a yellow perch. The fish's color not lost on me.

"If you had that kind of brass hat in your family . . . what?" I ask, throwing the fish back.

"Guess I'd be feelin' pretty darn conflicted too. Y'all been talkin' to anyone else?"

"Just my sister." I can divide everyone else in my life into three categories: people I can't tell; people I can't trust; people I can't burden.

"War hero and grandson of famous Iraq War general rejects Silver Star and refuses to return to the fight," Morpiss conjures a headline.

I picture a tow truck hauling that new Jeep Wrangler straight back to the dealer.

"There's a boatload of books and movies about the horrors of war," Morpiss points out. "It's in the news all the time. You'd have to be livin' under a rock not to know what war's like."

"Didn't stop you from signing up, did it?" I ask. "Didn't stop me. Maybe it's not real until it's a hundred and twenty degrees, you're humping eighty pounds of gear, there's sand in your eyes and crotch, and your heart's in your throat, staring down the barrel of an insurgent's AK."

"Ain't that the way it's always been?"

"People have always died of cancer. Doesn't mean you don't search for a cure."

"Well said." With his remaining hand, Morpiss slaps the arm of his wheelchair—his version of clapping, I guess.

Out in the lake, a fish jumps and splashes back down. The osprey takes flight, probably hoping the fish will jump again. You could argue that everyone in our country is safer because we've taken the fight over there instead of letting it come here.

Only, would it ever *really* come here? What country besides the United States has the ability to ship tens of thousands of troops anywhere in the world and keep them supplied?

As if he's read my thoughts, Morpiss says, "Here's where I think I come down on it, Jake. If y'all quit and speak out against the way this country mans its armies, it's gonna have a negative impact on a lot of people. A real hero makes sacrifices for his country. I ain't sayin' you ain't already done that. But who's to say where sacrifice ends?"

Spoken by someone who truly knows what the word "sacrifice" means.

In the bus back to Franklin the next afternoon, on the hot seat with the diesel fumes again. Looking out the window. The lush green countryside is so starkly different from the sun-blasted, war-ravaged landscape over there. Those listing, pockmarked, bombed-out buildings. The rubble and twisted rebar. But far worse than the destruction of the land was the destruction of the lives. Every village had gangs of small, malnourished orphans. Some missing limbs. They'd followed us everywhere, wanting to sell us candy or shine our shoes. Of course, they'd grow up to be warriors. War was all they knew.

I check my phone. We're back in the world of bars,

and there's another text from Brandi saying she wants to see me again. I admire her persistence, but I'm surprised. I thought I made it clear that I'm not going to appear in her video.

Of much more concern to me right now, there's still no word from Aurora or Erin Rose. I'm running out of time. I need to take a cue from Brandi and start trying harder.

BRAD

Light purple smoke filled the air. From the distance came the faint *whomp whomp* of the medevac bird. The medic had Morpiss on a stretcher a hundred yards down the road. Brad was keeping us away from him. Twenty minutes before, when they were bringing Morpiss down from the terrace, we heard the voices. The medic was trying to keep Morpiss from sinking into shock. "So what do you want the story to be? Land mine or RPG? If it was up to me, I'd go with RPG. It sounds more badass. That'll really impress the chicks."

It was the medic's job to make jokes. Trying to keep Morpiss distracted, even while the morphine dulled everything. It's what you were supposed to do. But they'd needed multiple tourniquets, so you had to hope there'd be a girl out there somewhere who would be impressed by a guy with no legs.

The medevac landed in a cloud of noise, wind, and

dust, and we watched them lift Morpiss aboard. The chopper took off, our buddy with it.

The faces around me were pale and drawn. Morpiss was done. The first in our squad to go. The first time most of us had seen someone be horribly wounded.

For life.

Nothing you thought you knew, nothing you'd imagined, prepared you for that.

Skitballs sat on his helmet, covered his face with his hands, and started to cry. The tears left tracks on his dark skin. I was fighting back tears myself. Someone lit a cigarette. We were still outside the wire, deep in enemy territory. I glanced at Brad, wondering why he hadn't ordered us to assemble.

But our squad leader just stood there with a grim look on his face, watching Skitballs sob. Finally, he went over, squatted beside the bawling soldier, put his arm around Skitballs's shoulders, and started to talk quietly. I wanted to go closer and listen in, but it felt like snooping, so I hung back with the others.

"Am I seeing things?" Magnet whispered.

"Another side of Sergeant Burrows, that's for sure," muttered Clay.

We waited, trying not to stare, while Brad consoled Skitballs. Finally, Lt. Abrams went over and said something. Brad and Skitballs got to their feet. The sappers were climbing back into the MRAP.

"Return to Base," Brad said. "Who wants to be the wheelman?"

"I will, Staff Sergeant," Magnet volunteered.

"No!" Clay and I shouted at the same time. For an instant, Magnet looked surprised. Then he got it.

Clay drove. Magnet and I sat in the back. No one manned the Browning. Clay and Magnet were the new guys in our squad. Both solid and dependable. Magnet, an inner-city kid from the south side of Chicago, who hoped he'd have a better chance of surviving in the Army than in a gang. Clay, a first-generation Hispanic American from El Paso, who saw the Army as a job opportunity. In the front, Brad slipped something under his tongue—one of the sublingual meds the docs gave out. He lit a cigarette. The Humvee bumped back to base.

"What about clearing the rest of the mines?" Skitballs asked.

"Now that a guy's been blowed up, they'll probably bring in the dogs," Clay grumbled.

Translation: Morpiss had to be torn to pieces for anyone up the chain of command to take the land mine problem seriously.

"Morpiss didn't have to be on that hill." The words came out of Brad in an anguished whisper. It was just me and him in his office. We'd returned from patrol about an hour ago.

"We had to provide support for the sappers, Sarge."

Brad suddenly exploded to his feet. The chair flew backward. He grabbed a can of Dr Pepper and hurled it against the map on the wall. Reddish-brown pop splashed out. The can clanked on the floor. "Glad you enlisted?" he shouted, face red, breathing hard. "Think Morpiss's glad? That he got used as a human mine detector because the XO didn't have a dog team to spare? Now he'll get to spend the rest of his life with no legs? And for what? Some stupid patch of dirt they wanted cleared so it can be used by a bunch of kids who are gonna grow up to hate us anyway."

I stood stock-still and stunned. There was no point in answering. The pop had spilled on his desk, on memos, on his keyboard, on a yellow legal pad covered with handwriting. Brad looked at the pop-splattered map. His shoulders drooped; his balled fists relaxed. He picked up the chair and sat, burying his face in his hands. "I can't take this anymore . . ." His shoulders trembled. He . . . he was *sobbing*. "I don't know what it is about this deployment. The first two I felt like I had a purpose. Couldn't wait to kill the bad guys. I was so gung-ho they practically had to tie me down. This time it's . . . it's like staring into blackness. All these ghosts in my head. All these blowed-off legs and arms. Bloody stumps and pieces of bodies."

My squad leader was blubbering. It was a startling, disturbing sight. I glanced at the door to make sure it was closed. To make sure no one else witnessed this. After a few moments, Brad seemed to get hold of himself. Wiped his eyes on his sleeve. "You swore, Private Liddell."

"Yes, Sarge, I remember. But, Sarge, what about speaking to combat stress control?"

Brad snorted derisively. "Sure. Or maybe I should just take a stroll outside the wire with my cammies down and let them shoot my balls off. Set foot in combat stress and you think I'll ever see another promotion? Staff Sergeant Bradley Burrows can't handle squad leader, so we'll kick him up to platoon leader. Now, that makes about as much sense as a screen door on a submarine."

"But, Sarge, if you're in this much misery . . ."

Brad straightened up and squared his shoulders. His eyebrows bunched into a scowl. Something about the word "misery" shook him out of it. He suddenly looked a lot more like a squad leader. "What did Erin Rose say about you, Private?"

I felt myself snap to attention. "I'm a standup guy, Sarge. None of that kiss-and-tell crap."

"That's correct, Private. Know what I'm going to say next?"

"Yes, Sarge. You're going to say, 'Get your punk private first class ass out of here.'"

"Correct." He turned back to his desk and started blotting the wet papers.

I headed for the door, then stopped. "Sarge?"

"What?" Brad growled as if he was annoyed I was still there.

"We're all broke up about Morpiss, but you did what you were supposed to do. It's not your fault."

Brad let the papers fall to his desk. He leaned back in his chair and stared up at the ceiling. "Tell that to his legs. And get the hell out."

AURORA

She's waiting for me at the bus station. Emotion wells up in my heart. I'm super glad she's here. She must have called Lori to find out what time I'd be coming in. We hug and share a brief kiss.

"I don't want it to end," she whispers.

"Neither do I." Boy, do I mean it.

The only way I can get my cast into her beat-up Toyota Corolla is by sliding the seat all the way back and then tilting it almost as far as it will go. I'm reclining so far back I'm looking at the ceiling. It's amazing that this old beater still runs. The dashboard is sun-cracked and the speedometer is shot. The windshield has spidery fissures and the check-engine light has been on since the day she got it.

While Aurora drives, I reach over and gently twist a lock of her soft hair around my finger. We've been together since junior year. I'm the only real serious boyfriend she's ever had.

"How's your friend?" she asks.

The spell is broken. It's not her fault. It was bound to happen. But, do I tell her the truth? "He's . . . okay."

The sharp glance she gives me says she knows I'm not telling the truth. "Why can't you tell me?"

"Aurora . . ."

"You used to tell me everything."

Sure. Back when we were innocent high school kids without a clue. Before I went over there. Before there was so much that I wish I didn't know and had never seen.

"Jake, it's not going to work if you can't be honest with me," she says.

I feel myself grow tense. I could say the same to her. *How're things with Doug Rhinebach?* But that wouldn't be fair. Because, according to her friend Emily, there really isn't any "thing" between Aurora and Doug.

"If what happened to him had happened to me, it wouldn't work between us anyway," I tell her.

She gives me a quick, cold frown. "You think I'm that shallow?"

"No, that's not what I meant. It wouldn't work because I wouldn't let it work. You deserve better."

Her face scrunches. I'm being obtuse. "Okay, you *really* want to know how my friend is? He lost both of his legs and some of the lower area of his body. And his left arm. All he's got is part of his body, his head, and one arm. He lives in a shack in the woods a million miles from everything with no one to take care of him except his mother. The only things left for him are fishing and vaping."

Aurora stares ahead and blinks. We pass the McDonald's. The big sign out front says, HAPPY 98TH BIRTHDAY, WOODY! Welcoming home the war hero is old news. We pass the Pizza Hut, the World War I memorial with its rusty wagon-wheeled cannon and doughboys in their wide-brimmed helmets. Thirty-eight *million* people died in that war. Soldiers. Civilians. Women, and children. The military tries to dehumanize the murder of unarmed civilians by calling it collateral damage. Damage. Like what happens when your car bangs into a tree. But it isn't damage. It's death. And giving it a different name makes no difference to anyone who has seen it up close. Until you've been to war yourself, you can't even begin to comprehend what that means. *How that feels.* It's not the number. It's the utter misery. In war, you learn that those who die instantly are the lucky ones. The rest suffer terrible pain and agony. And not just from their wounds. They die of hunger, or thirst, or disease. All endure the worst kind of fear and terror imaginable.

And for what?

"I'm . . . I'm sorry about your friend," Aurora says.

It's not just Morpiss. It's every human being who's ever died because of war. Who's ever been wounded and maimed. And not just physically, but mentally, too.

Aurora pulls up in front of my house, but neither of us gets out of the car. We sit in silence, not knowing what to say. It's like the other night at the end of our "private" road in the woods. Like she's just asked if she should wait for me.

Should she wait for a guy who's supposed to go away again for another six months? And if he does go, may never come back? Or may come back far more physically or mentally damaged than I am now?

And if I decide not to go back? If I say to the Army, "Take your medal and shove it. Because no matter what you do to me, it can't be as bad as war."

Where would that leave Aurora? Does she want to be with a guy who's brought shame to his family? To his town? To the entire military?

Neither option looks particularly promising. If I really love her, maybe the best thing I can do is help her cut her losses and start over with someone new. Someone like Doug Rhinebach, heir to the Rhinebach Auto Group.

A curtain in our living room draws back. Someone looks out. The curtain closes.

In the car, Aurora and I stare straight ahead. She's waiting for me to say something.

What can I say when I don't know what I'm doing? When no matter what I do, chances are it will hurt her?

I hear a sniff. A tear rolls down Aurora's cheek. She reaches for the key and starts the engine.

"I'm sorry, sweetheart." It's all I can say.

Then it's time for me to get out.

Lying in bed in the dark. It's probably around 2 a.m. My mind is racing.

I don't want to lose Aurora. But I can't deceive her. If I go back over there, I'm not as worried about getting killed as I am coming back with missing parts. That's not what she signed up for. It's not what she should have to feel obligated to spend the rest of her life dealing with.

And what about Erin Rose? I can't wait any longer for an answer to my texts and emails. Tomorrow I'm going to have to track her down.

And then there's my family.

And my future.

All these thoughts racing around and around. Guess it's a good thing I've still got some no-goes. The Army provides soldiers with a selection. The short-term variety gets you about four hours of shut-eye. The medium-term pill is good for six. And then there's Sleeping Beauty, a twelve-hour sleep-like-a-baby dose that leaves you feeling the next morning like you've been raised from the dead.

None of it's the over-the-counter stuff you can buy at Walgreens. It's all heavy-duty prescription meds, the kinds that come with lots of red-and-yellow warning labels. You almost have to take them to fight this kind of war. You need to sleep, so you take a no-go. But when your body gets used to one pill, you have to take two no-goes to sleep. And you're doing the same thing with pain meds and anti-anxiety meds. Guys taking that stuff wake up in the morning feeling like their brains are clogged with sludge. So they take a go pill. That plus battery acid and Rip-It and you're good and wired and ready for action.

It became a cycle. Pretty soon guys had so many meds inside them that they couldn't think straight, couldn't feel straight. So what did the docs do? Gave them anti-depressants and anti-psychotics to stop all the other meds from driving them crazy. After a while, guys were taking seven or eight different pills a day. With no one monitoring them. No one to say, hey man, it can't be good to take so many medications at once. Maybe you should try to get off some of this stuff.

Usually you could tell who was on the heavy cocktails. They'd develop weird tics, or forget what you'd just said to them, or fly into a rage over nothing. There were stories of guys getting paranoid, guys going on shooting sprees. And, of course, guys so whacked out they did themselves in.

For tonight, the medium six-hour dose will probably be the best. I'll need to be bright-eyed and bushy-tailed in the morning. There's still a lot to do.

THE GENERAL

rack! Crack! Crack! I go code red and start to drop, but a gnarled, bony hand grabs my arm. "Easy, son. It's just some firecrackers."

The hand belongs to Howard Miller, sitting next to me in his old olive Special Forces uniform. We're on the back of the General's white 1975 Eldorado convertible, his parade car. Old Howie is another of Franklin's military heroes. From Vietnam. He's been in parades before.

I take a slug from a water bottle and try to swallow down my racing heart. What is a parade? A convoy. I know there are no IEDs planted along Main Street, but when those firecrackers went off, I automatically reacted. *Sniper!*

"Keep waving, son," Old Howie says out of the corner of his smile. The sun-washed street is lined with people wearing hats and sunglasses. Some wave American flags. Others shade their eyes with their hands. I'm still trembling from the aftershock of the firecrackers. Maybe I should have taken an anti-anxiety pill for this parade. But I'm trying to break the habit.

I know how Old Howie deals with the stress. Just before the parade began, I walked into the bathroom in the firehouse and found him filling his empty water bottle from a flask. *Vashe zdorovie*, Howie!

Pop! Pop! Pop! I'm prepared when the next set of firecrackers explodes. But I still get tense. Can't help it. I don't know who originally thought that a good way to honor military vets was with a parade and fireworks. But it had to be someone who'd never been in battle.

The parade ends at Town Hall with a round of speeches. I've been told ahead of time that I won't be asked to speak. I'm just on display. All I have to do is accept a gold-plated key to the city and say thank you.

Then it's off to Anthony's, the best steak house in town and the General's favorite hangout. In fact, the General likes the place so much that about ten years ago, when it ran into financial trouble because people weren't eating as much steak as they used to, he bought an interest in it just to keep it going.

Our family sits at a big round table. Now and then during the meal, someone comes over from another table to say hello to the General and congratulate me. Then, just before dessert I look up and see Brandi standing inside the front door. When she catches my eye, she tilts her head to the left and disappears from sight.

I pretend I need to use the john. Brandi's waiting for me by the ladies' room.

"Had a feeling you'd be here after the parade," she says. "Can we talk some more?"

"I told you, I can't be in that video."

"That's not what I'm talking about."

"Then what *are* you talking about?"

Her eyes slide toward the dining room, as if implying that what she wants to say could take a while.

"Not sure how long I'll be," I tell her.

"I'll wait in the park."

I return to my family feeling conflicted. If not about the video, what does Brandi want to talk about? Why didn't I just say no?

At the table, the General's telling the same old war stories we've all heard a hundred times before. The ones that always start out as tales about the funny or stupid thing someone else did or said, but somehow always end with my grandfather looking like a hero. My father sits quietly and hardly says a word, just as he always does at family meals with the General.

Dinner's over when the General says it is. Then he announces that he and I are going to stay behind and have a little chat. Dad gives me a nod. Lori says she'll see me at the house later. Everyone departs.

"What are you drinking?" the General asks me while a busboy clears the table.

I'm a tequila man, but in the General's company, it's

the rule of bourbon. The only choice you have is which brand. "Jim Beam Signature, sir. On the rocks."

"Good choice." The General tells the waiter to make it two. My being underage isn't an issue. He's the General and part owner of this establishment. There's not a law officer within a hundred miles of Franklin who would think of citing this restaurant for serving me.

"Heard you visited a squad buddy yesterday," he says while we wait for our drinks.

How does he know that? Does he have a staffer draw up a daily report of his family's whereabouts? "Yes, sir."

"WIA?"

"Yes, sir. Pretty bad. Lost both legs and an arm."

The General shakes his head slowly. "The bane of modern warfare. When I was a soldier, men like that didn't survive. Who knows whether it's a good thing now that they do?"

The waiter delivers our drinks.

"To your future." The General lifts his rock glass.

We toast. The bourbon goes down hot and cold.

"A moment like this calls for a good Cuban cigar," the General says with a sigh but leaves it at that. "Son, I know your deployment isn't over and you're going into rehab so you can go back over there. That's not only admirable and what a hero should do, but exactly what I'd expect of you. Only, I'm arranging for you to attend Officer Candidate School at Fort Benning first. It's clear that you possess the kind of bravery and leadership skills we need in the Army. Once you've completed the twelve-week course, you'll be able to return to the front lines as a second lieutenant. With your own platoon to lead. And I'm confident you'll continue to rise through the ranks from there."

While I didn't expect him to say this, I can't say I'm surprised.

He pauses for a moment, then displays one of his rare smiles. "I can't begin to tell you how proud I am of the way you've conducted yourself."

"I appreciate it, sir. But aren't I kind of young to be a commissioned officer? I doubt the more experienced NCOs under my command would take kindly to being ordered around by a twenty-year-old."

The General's forehead wrinkles. He gives me a perplexed look. "Son, you are being considered for the Silver Star for conspicuous gallantry in action. The soldiers under your command will regard you with nothing short of the well-deserved awe and respect you have earned."

I lift my rock glass and consider the amber liquid inside. The General isn't *asking* if I want to become an officer. This is an *order*.

"I've started the paperwork," he says. "When you get to Walter Reed, there'll be a packet with your application and other information waiting for you."

He picks up his glass and knocks back the rest of his drink in one gulp, then checks his watch and starts to rise.

"I'd like to stay and chat, son, but I've got to get home. Need a ride somewhere?"

"Uh, thanks, but I'm meeting someone."

He hesitates for a moment, then smiles and gives me a soft punch on the shoulder. "Atta boy."

BRANDI

The setting sun is a low yellow glare in my eyes as I walk toward the park. I feel a little unsteady. I forgot that at Anthony's when the General orders a bourbon, it's automatically a double.

Brandi's sitting on a bench, texting. In the dusky light, some families are still playing with their kids on the swings and plastic tube slide.

"So how's your famous grandfather?" Brandi asks when I sit down.

"Why did you come?" I ask.

"I feel like we haven't finished talking. And you've been avoiding me," she says. "Which makes me think there's more to discuss."

She gets me with those X-ray eyes again. Like she can see right through me.

"You're supposed to ask, 'Like what?'" she says.

Suddenly I wish I hadn't had that bourbon. I need to

be on my game around her. "Maybe this isn't such a good idea. I really should—"

She presses her hand down on my right thigh, the one that's not in the cast. She slides a little closer. "Did you have friends who died over there?"

Why did she have to ask that? Outside the Army, I might never have had the opportunity to become friends with Morpiss and Skitballs and the rest. We came from different parts of the country, different ethnic and social backgrounds, different religions. But in uniform, none of that mattered. We depended on each other for our lives. We needed each other to survive. We were brothers. "Yes."

"Minorities?"

"Some."

"Then you know what I've been talking about, Jake. People like your buddies. People who shouldn't have to die just because they're underprivileged and don't have choices. You agree with that, don't you?"

"What do you think? Of course I do. I just don't understand why—"

She raises a hand. "Hear me out. You said you don't feel comfortable being in the video, but what if—"

A flashbang goes off in my head. I can't believe I didn't think of this sooner. "Where's your phone?"

"What?" Brandi straightens.

"I want to see your phone." She was holding it when I got here, but now it's out of sight.

"Why?"

"Are you recording this?"

"What? No!"

"Then let me see it."

"No."

"Seriously? Now I *really* want to see it."

Her bag is lying on the bench between us.

We both have the same idea.

But I'm faster.

"Stop!" she cries, grabbing my arm. But her protest isn't really angry. It's half laughter. I open the bag and reach in. Her hands squeeze my wrist. "I said stop! You can't do this. You're violating my space!" But still, she's almost laughing.

And strangely enough, so am I. "Oh yeah? Well, you're violating my . . . my right to not be recorded without prior warning." I pull her phone out. Of course, it's locked. Now she's trying to wrestle the phone out of my grasp. But it's more of a play struggle than a real one. And obviously, she knows I can't open it anyway. So why are we locked in this pretend battle?

"Want to see how I used to beat my brother in arm wrestling?" She grabs my hand with both of hers and throws her bare shoulder into me. I smell her fresh sweet fragrance. Suddenly our "meeting" is going in a really strange direction.

I let her have the phone, but she's still leaning into me, breathing hard. We're practically lying together on the bench. Our faces are only inches apart. Our eyes meet and I sense that she too is wondering what, exactly, is going on.

She retreats, sits up on the bench, and straightens her clothes. We're still catching our breath.

"Seriously, you're not supposed to record someone without them knowing," I tell her.

"I wasn't."

"Then why wouldn't you let me see the phone?"

"Because it's mine, and if I don't want you touching my stuff, then you shouldn't."

"So that's what this was all about? Me touching your stuff?"

"And going into my bag. Is that something you do a lot? Just randomly go into girls' bags without their permission?"

"Oh yeah, all the time. Just can't stay out of them."

It's twilight. The families are starting to drift away from the playground. Now that Brandi's regained control of her phone, she unlocks it and shows me that there's nothing on the recording app with today's date on it.

"Happy?" she asks.

No, I'm feeling anything but happy. The air between us is still charged. And the thing about electrical charges is, sometimes they repel, but sometimes they attract. And I can't help wondering if this has something to do with the very shaky state of my relationship with Aurora right now.

But all of that is off topic. Only I'm having a hard time remembering exactly what the topic was. *Damn that Jim Beam Signature.*

"We were talking about you not wanting to be in the video," Brandi reminds me.

Right. I take a couple of deep breaths and try to focus. What just happened was way too weird. I have to regroup and shift gears from this immediate and very physical "interaction" with Brandi. Back to the JROTC video. "I told you why I can't be in it."

"What if you were only in silhouette?" she asks. "And we disguised your voice?"

"Something like, 'Recent Franklin High graduate, grandson of famous Army general, and wounded war hero who doesn't want his identity revealed'? Gee, I bet no one would have a clue." I'm not a big fan of sarcasm, but sometimes it's unavoidable.

Brandi looks off across the playground, a place where American children play with no idea of the brutality and hardships children in other parts of the world endure. *There has never been a war in which children haven't suffered and died.*

Brandi's shoulders slump. "You're right. If I say anything about your grandfather or what happened to you over there, then everyone will know. But if I don't mention those things, then it doesn't have to be you. It could be anyone who served over there."

Her disappointment is palpable. I can't help feeling bad for her.

She gathers herself. "Jake, you know that there's a story here. And it needs to be told by someone whose opinion matters. There has to be a way you can do it. Tell the world that we really don't have an all-volunteer Army. We've just changed the method of conscription. We let economic forces compel minorities and have-nots to gamble their bodies and lives for a slim shot at a better financial future. That's not fair, Jake. You and I both know it. Won't you do something?"

How can you not be impressed? This isn't some wannabe YouTube star trying to draw attention to herself by creating a controversial video. It doesn't look like she even wants to be in the video. She just wants to do something for a great many innocent young Americans who aren't aware of how those in power want to use them.

I break the silence. "I admire your determination, Brandi. Seriously. I mean, having the guts to stand up for something you believe in and know is going to be unpopular. Especially here in Franklin."

And I'm thinking: *She has more guts than you appear to have, Jake.*

Why should it be the poor and minorities, the disadvantaged and luckless, who have to bear the burden of risking their lives for our country? And it's not just them. It's guys like me who are seduced by the action ads and unethical recruiters. Guys who believe that enlisting is their duty and obligation to their country. I could have so easily avoided all of this. Could have gone to college, gotten a job. Could have chosen a life where the worst scars come from a burn I get while cooking burgers on the outdoor grill. Where the worst nightmare is a scrape on my new car.

It's getting dark. Brandi hasn't said a word. Meanwhile,

there are things I still need to do. "Well, I—"

Before I can make an excuse for going, she squeezes my arm. "You didn't answer my question. Won't you do something?"

In the dimming light her eyes are dark and not so penetrating. Will we ever figure out the answers? Why we need to have armies? Why we need to go to war?

I take a deep breath. There *is* something I can do.

ERIN ROSE

could have asked Aurora's friends if they knew Erin Rose's new address, but I didn't want them telling Aurora I was going to visit my old girlfriend. It was Barry, the bartending bassist with the Zombie Horde, who knew where to find her.

The address is a few towns over. I take an Uber to a sprawling ranch house with a brick facade and large, neatly trimmed lawn. I ring the doorbell and wait. A vacuum hums inside. When no one comes to the door, I ring again.

The vacuum stops. "Who is it?" a voice calls.

"Jake Liddell, ma'am. I'm a friend of Mrs. Burrows."

"I think you must have the wrong house," the voice says.

"Erin Rose Burrows?"

The door opens an inch. A young woman peeks out. "You mean, Erin Rose Dixon?"

She's gone back to her maiden name. "Sorry. Yes, that's who I mean."

She gives me a look up and down as if she's not sure what to do.

"I'm a friend of her husband. Former husband. From the Army."

The young woman scowls at me. "You sure we're talking about the same person?"

What's this? How can she work here and not know that Erin Rose had a husband in the Army? There's a stroller in the front hall. "She has a daughter, Amber? Probably about two and a half years old?"

The young woman nods and seems uncertain about what to do.

"If you want to check with her, I'll wait."

For some reason, this offer helps put her at ease. She points. "She's out in the back. You can go around the house."

I let myself through a gate, crutch it past a swimming pool and grilling island large enough to cook for a squad. Farther out in the yard, Erin Rose is hanging sheets on an outdoor clothes tree. She's cut her dark hair to shoulder length, and her biceps have more definition than I remember. She must go to the gym a lot. Amber, small and dark-haired, is pulling at some laundry in a basket on the ground.

Erin Rose sees me, stops what she's doing, then bends down and picks up her daughter. They both watch me approach.

"I knew you'd come," she says without a smile. Not the warmest of welcomes. Amber tugs at her mother's hair.

"You remember Jake, don't you?" Erin Rose asks her daughter. Amber shakes her head and hides her face. "I'm sure she does. She's just being shy."

Amber peeks out, points at my cast.

"He got hurt, sweetheart." Erin Rose turns to me. "So I hear you're a hero. Congratulations." Still no smile. She's wary. Cautious. Defensive.

"Thanks."

It's been more than a year since we've seen each other. Doesn't seem to matter now that for years we were sweethearts and then close friends. She's clearly uncomfortable with me being there.

"So I take it you have something to say to me," Erin Rose says. She looks back at the house. The young woman who greeted me in the front is standing inside the sliding glass doors, watching. Erin Rose waves to her and she comes out.

"Would you like something?" Erin Rose asks me.

"No, thanks. I'm fine."

The young woman arrives and Erin Rose hands Amber off with a kiss and a promise that she'll be in the house to see her soon. The breeze rustles the hanging sheets.

"I've always loved the smell of air-dried sheets," Erin Rose says, watching the young woman carry her daughter away.

"Should we sit?" I ask.

"I suppose."

We cross the yard to a table under an umbrella beside

the pool. The filter gurgles. The breeze pushes an inflatable white-and-black swan across the surface.

"Nice place," I tell her.

Erin Rose reads more into the statement than I intended. "When Brad went into the Army, he was away more than he was home. People don't get married and then stop getting to know each other. My girlfriends say it never stops. But with Brad, the more he was away, the less I felt I knew him."

"Erin, I'm not here to make you feel defensive," I tell her.

Her eyebrows dip.

"Isn't there supposed to be a year between deployments?" I ask.

Erin Rose smirks. "They have ways to get around that, especially when they're not making their recruitment goals. And anyway, after his first deployment, Brad couldn't wait to go back over there. He pulled strings and went early for extra training. The same thing after his second deployment. That's the one that really threw me, because it wasn't just me he was leaving, but Amber. We had really bad fights. He kept saying he couldn't help himself. He just didn't feel normal here. He couldn't figure out what to do with himself when he was home. But it made me so angry that he was in a rush to leave Amber."

She grows quiet. Alone with her thoughts, I guess. But when she looks at me, her eyes are brimming with tears. "I know you and he got close over there. Do you hate me now?"

I shake my head and put my hand on hers. "No, not at all. What happened wasn't your fault."

She wipes the tears away. "They wouldn't fly him home on the same plane with the KIAs. Like he didn't deserve the same treatment. They sent him home on a different plane, alone. There was no one waiting for him when he got here."

So different from the welcome I received. And yet, there was hardly any difference between Brad and me. We were both soldiers, trying our best to serve our country. Both badly wounded by war.

"But you got the death benefit, right?"

She sniffs and nods. "It's for Amber's college."

The young woman comes out with a tray. A pitcher of tea and two glasses filled with ice. Erin Rose may have wiped the tears away, but her eyes are still red. The young woman sees this and scowls while she places the tray on the table.

"Thank you, Stacy," Erin Rose says. "What's Amber doing?"

"Watching *Curious George*."

"Not too much TV, okay?"

Stacy nods and heads back toward the house. Erin Rose pours the iced tea. She smiles sadly at me. "It's nice to see you, Jake."

"You too, Erin."

She takes a sip of tea and gazes out across the yard. It's at least an acre. A good place to raise children. Her eyes well up again. "He said you were a good friend. The only one he could talk to."

"He was a fine soldier. He did his best for his men."

She frowns. "You wrote that there were things you wanted to say, but had to say in person . . ."

"He blamed himself," I tell her. "He knew he scared you. He knew he hadn't been a good husband. Like you said, he couldn't help himself. It was like he'd become addicted to the action. And to the brotherhood."

She screws up her face. "Then why did he . . . ?"

"He wasn't right in the head. You knew about all the meds, right? It was like an ogre inside him. Another creature he had to do battle against."

She nods sadly. "He took a lot of pills when he was home, too."

"It wasn't just him. A lot of guys had that ogre stomping around inside their heads. You knew Brad. Before he enlisted, there was nothing that would have made him take his own life. Not in a million years. But you mix what war does to you with those drugs, and it's lethal."

"But he knew about Garth. He knew I was leaving him . . ."

"Like I said, Erin. He blamed himself. He started to blame himself for everything."

Erin Rose wipes more tears from her eyes. "I was afraid you were going to tell me it was my fault. That he wouldn't have killed himself if I hadn't left him."

The white bedsheets flap in the afternoon breeze. In the house, Amber comes to the sliding glass door and presses her forehead against it. She waves and Erin Rose waves back. That little girl is all that remains of Brad, a man who gave his life for his country just like any so-called hero.

BRAD

Ka-boom! The explosion was so big and close that the shock waves knocked a few guys out of their beds. The air was instantly filled with dust. Ears ringing painfully, I started to feel around for a light amid shouts and coughing in the dark.

"What the hell?"

"Must've hit right outside," Skitballs said.

Everyone was hacking, grabbing for anything they could find to press over their noses and mouths to keep the dust out of their lungs.

Clay was the first to find a light. "Wasn't a rocket. There was no siren."

But the words had hardly left his lips when the sirens started. The knee-jerk reaction was to run for the nearest bunker, but everyone stopped at half stride when the siren cut out, then started and stopped again. That code had been drilled into us.

"Attack!" Magnet shouted.

The small arms fire began. Then *bang, floosh, boom!* An RPG. Then the crack of more shots and small arms. We pulled on our armor as fast as we could.

The barracks door banged open and Brad stuck his head in. "SVBIED at the front gate! They're coming in!"

Then he was gone.

The huge blast had been a truck loaded with explosives crashing into the front gate. The small-arms fire and booms of RPGs were the insurgents piling in through the gap where the front gate had been. Outside through the drifting smoke and dust, it was just starting to get light. The firefight was on. We heard the rip of Brad's SAW and headed toward it, scrambling from barracks to Conex boxes to T-walls, skirting and tripping over smoking debris thrown a hundred yards by the explosion.

Bullets whizzed and pocked into walls. Men shouted. Peeking around the corner of a Conex, I saw Brad crouched behind a pile of sandbags, shooting at an upward angle. It didn't make sense until we saw the muzzle flashes of returning fire. The insurgents had gotten into the gate guard tower. They were firing down on us. We were pinned down inside our own FOB.

Brad waved us over. A moment later, Skitballs, Clay, and I were hunkered beside him behind the sandbags.

"Take the SAW." Brad handed Clay the machine gun. He tapped me on the helmet. "Clay and Skit'll cover us. We're going there." He pointed at the corner of a barracks halfway between the sandbags and the guard tower.

I felt my scrotum contract. Even with suppressive fire, we'd be running right under the insurgents' noses.

Clay and Skitballs started firing. I followed Brad, running as fast as my legs would carry me, praying I wouldn't get hit. Lead whizzed past us and kicked up dirt around our feet. Breathing hard, we reached the side of the barracks and pressed our backs against the wall. Clay and Skitballs had ceased fire and were safe behind the sandbags while the insurgents kept firing, wasting their ammo. We could always hope they'd shoot their weapons dry.

"How many frags you got?" Brad yelled over the pops and bangs.

"Two, Sarge."

"Okay, that makes four. How's your aim?"

"Guess we'll see, Sarge. Where're we gonna deliver from?"

"On the run, soldier."

If my scrotum felt tight before, now my balls felt like they'd crawled up into my throat. The guard tower was open on four sides. But throw too low and the frag grenade would hit the lower wall and bounce back at us. Throw too high and it would bounce off the roof and roll back on us. In other words, if our aim wasn't perfect, we were more likely to kill ourselves than the enemy.

"Ready?" Brad grinned tightly. It was one of those moments when I felt like he was testing me. Like trying to see if I'd been man enough for Erin Rose.

Or maybe he was testing himself.

"Ready, Sarge." My M-16 was strapped and I had a frag grenade in each hand.

Brad signaled Clay and Skitballs for more suppressive fire, then he and I took off across the open yard. When we got close enough, we threw the grenades. Luckily, our aim was good. The first two landed inside the guard tower.

That's when it hit me that Brad had forgotten one important part of the plan. Once we'd thrown the grenades, then what? We were out in the open. Brad tackled me and we both hit the ground.

Boom!

I half expected the tower to fall on us. Next thing I knew, Brad was on his feet, yanking me back up. He had his handgun out. "Come on!" He signaled Clay and Skitballs and headed up the guard tower ladder.

The scene inside the tower was gruesome. Mangled bodies, blood, parts of bodies. The acrid stink of smoke. Clay and Skitballs joined us. More insurgents were pushing up the road and through the wire. Some found cover behind rocks or small rises of dirt. Others were out in the open. We made quick work of the ones who weren't well protected. But the ones that had found cover kept firing.

In the distance, a car was racing parallel to the wire, leaving a long cloudy trail of yellow dust. It turned and came tearing up the road toward the blown-out gate. This was another SVBIED for sure. Clay got the car in the

SAW's sights and let loose. The windshield turned white, then blew in. The driver got smoked. The car slowed and came to a stop about thirty yards from the front gate.

The insurgents turned their fire from us to the car.

"Aw—" Brad started to curse.

Ka-boom!

We were knocked backward. The car had been loaded with explosives. The insurgents fired at it to ignite them. Ears ringing, heads throbbing, we got back to our positions just in time to see the last heated-up RPG rounds launch in crazy directions from the flaming wreckage like the finale of a fireworks display.

And then came the kids.

Three of them in baggy camos and sneakers, lugging AKs and running up the road toward the gate. Almost all the fire from our side stopped as we stared, aghast at the sight. They were skinny, all knees and elbows, not even old enough to have whiskers. The legs and sleeves of their camos had been rolled up.

"Got to be kidding," Clay muttered.

We silently hoped the warning shots Brad fired over their heads would be enough to make them turn tail. Instead, two took knees and fired while the third kept coming.

They'd been trained.

One of their shots smacked into a corner post of the guard tower not a foot from Skitballs's head.

When we still didn't return fire, the other two jumped to their feet and started toward us again. By now the first kid was just passing the smoldering skeleton of the SVBIED. He was the smallest of the three. Probably the youngest. Twelve? Thirteen? Carrying an AK.

What the hell do you do?

In the guard tower, Brad reached for my M-16. He looked grim. "Your weapon, Private."

I let him take it.

The next couple of days around the FOB were pretty busy. The two guys who'd originally been manning the guard tower had been killed by the first SVBIED, and three others were pretty badly wounded in the subsequent firefight. We had a memorial service and did a lot of patrol work to reestablish the perimeter. Buildings had to be repaired and the front gate rebuilt.

But no matter how busy they kept us, the memory of those kids was never far from my thoughts. We all knew that they shouldn't have been involved. They should have been in school or outside playing. They had no idea what was at stake. When my friends and I were their age, we'd gone to war too. With toy guns. We got shot, fell down, and then got right back up again. You had to wonder if death was any more real to those child soldiers who'd attacked us than it was to us at that age.

Everyone in the squad knew why Brad had used my M-16. He didn't want any of us to take the responsibility. He wanted to do it in one clean shot. The SAW would have made a mess of the body. The other two kids were also dusted. But that was a few seconds later when the firefight erupted again. No one knew for sure who'd done it.

The deaths of those kids got to me in a way little else in that stupid war had, but I kept it inside. I'm certain it weighed on some of the others, too. Brad never said a word, but I know it got to him. By then he and I were pretty tight. I knew that Erin Rose had filed for divorce. Strangely, Brad didn't seem that broken up about it. He said that it was probably for the best. That he didn't think he had it in him to be a good husband and father. Maybe I should have listened more carefully or thought more about what he'd said. About what state his mind must have been in to say things like that.

About what state his mind was in to volunteer to be the one who smoked that kid. Knowing he'd have to live with that for the rest of his life.

AURORA

'm driving the Jeep to her parents' house. I sure hope there isn't a law against operating a vehicle while part of your leg in a cast is sticking out of the gap where the removable door usually is. In less than twenty-four hours, I either leave for Walter Reed or turn my world upside down. It's after five o'clock, and Aurora's not answering my texts or calls. The clock ticks. I may not know what decision I'll make, but I do know I don't want to lose her.

Maybe I've been stupid. Maybe I've tried to be too fair by giving her an out. But like some cowboy once said, "You don't miss your water till your well runs dry." Without Aurora these past few days, it feels like my well is parched.

I manage to get to the house without getting pulled over by the cops. But Aurora's Corolla isn't in the driveway. Now what? Do I just drive around town looking for her?

No.

I turn around and head home, feeling pretty low. Maybe

this was a dumb idea anyway. Maybe it's too late for Aurora and me.

The ride home takes me along Lakeside Drive. It's a typical hot early-summer day and people are out on the lake on paddleboards and kayaks. Stopped at a traffic light, I watch a ski boat race past.

What I see next makes me blink with astonishment. The water-skier is Aurora.

When did she learn to waterski?

The car behind me honks. How long has the light been green? I pull to the curb and watch the ski boat carve a wide circle and then pass again. Even from here you can see the big smile on Aurora's face. Should I wait? Or should I go back home and call her later?

While I'm debating this, the ski boat slows. Aurora lets go of the towline and glides until she sinks down. The boat comes around and stops beside her. Doug Rhinebach reaches over the side and helps her climb in.

BRAD

t's my last night at home. The hospital bed is no longer in the den, but the mail crates loaded with letters are, along with the manila envelope filled with phone numbers and messages. Even if I find the time someday to reply to all of them, will I know what to say?

Lori and Dad make a great meal, but it's consumed in an air of gloom. Lori gets teary. By not making a decision, it looks like I've made one. Tomorrow I'll be heading for Walter Reed. And after that? Officer Candidate School at Fort Benning, I guess.

Halfway through dinner, my phone vibrates. It's a text. From Erin Rose: Snt u email.

That's strange.

After dinner I go up to my room and read it:

Dear Jake,
I'm really glad you came by. I was afraid of what you

might say, but as always, you were a true gentleman. Thank you so much for that. I've attached the last letter I got from Brad. I've often wondered why he wrote it out on paper instead of just sending it as an email. I think maybe he wanted me to have something I could hold in my hands. Maybe something I could share with Amber when she's old enough. Anyway, when you were here, I wasn't sure whether to show it to you or not. I didn't have time to think about it. But now I've thought it over. I don't think Brad would have minded me showing it to you. And again, thank you for understanding.

Love,
ER

I click on the attachment. It's a scan of a letter written on yellow-lined paper. The paper is wrinkled, with reddish stains. So this was what Brad was writing in his office the night he hurled the Dr Pepper at the wall. It's smudged in spots as if it's been read and reread dozens of times. Knowing Erin Rose, I'm sure it has.

Dear Erin Rose,
I'm writing this because I can't take it anymore.
Every day is torture, and it only gets worse. Its been going on for a long time.
Its constant agony. I'm not even sure where the

physical pain ends and the mental begins. Its all mixed together. Every day is a waking nightmare. Horrible memories, guilt, anxiety. The meds used to help a little . . . for a while . . . but I feel like now they just scramble my brains and add to the depression, doubt, and pain.

The things I did on my first two deployments haunt me.

A couple of weeks ago at Airbase Delta, I ran into the guy we used to call Fozzy. He and I served together during my first deployment. Our eyes met, and we both looked away. Passed each other and never said a word.

I know what he was thinking because I was thinking it too. About the things we were ordered to do. The things we had to do. To get information. To kill the enemy before they killed us. To survive. Thats all it ever was. Just trying to survive. I can't even remember if it was ever about winning this stupid war.

No matter what anyone says, you can't play fair against an enemy that doesn't play fair. Against an enemy that dies willingly. I was guarding a checkpoint and this young woman came toward us carrying a bundle. We yelled at her to stop, but she kept coming. Not running, but coming steadily. Suicide bombers are a real problem. They mix in with a crowd of GIs and blow themselves up and take half a dozen guys with them.

We kept yelling and waving, but she wouldn't stop. Soon she was going to be close enough to the checkpoint to blow us all up.

Everyone knew what had to be done, but no one wanted to be the one who did it. But someone had to take the shot. I guess I thought I'd be a hero. Not because I'd shoot an unarmed woman, but because I'd spare my fellow soldiers the awful task.

I fired and she went down. We were waiting to see what would happen next when the bundle she was carrying moved.

I wanted to puke.

A couple of guys took a closer look. She was carrying an infant. The kid had been badly burned, probably thanks to one of our artillery attacks or bombing raids. She was probably bringing him to us for help.

Now, not only did we burn the kid. We killed his mother.

I wish that was the only thing. But it wasn't. There was a lot. Some things we were ordered to do. Things that would be considered war crimes in any military court. None of us wanted to do them. But we had no choice. To refuse was to endanger the lives of your fellow soldiers.

So I did them. Lots of us did. I don't know how the other guys dealt with it. But now all those things are in me, always. I can't escape. Sometimes I think only a crazy person could live with the things we had to do.

Maybe thats the problem. I feel crazy now, but maybe not crazy enough.

You must be wondering, if it was that bad, why would I ever go back for a second deployment? And then a third? The answer is that after the first deployment I felt guilty about what I'd done. I went back for the second because I stupidly thought that maybe I could do a better job. I felt I owed it to all the soldiers who died, and to those who were still alive. I told myself that if I did better this time, the ghosts that were haunting me would go away.

Maybe I did do a little better during that second deployment. But people still died. Our enemies were still being tortured and murdered. And the ghosts from the first deployment were still there.

And the third deployment? I think you know why I went. By then I couldn't live with myself, or you and Amber. I was going crazy at home. You knew because you walked into the bathroom and I was sitting there with a gun in my mouth. You have no idea how many times I did that when you didn't walk in. I had to come back here so that whatever I did, I wouldn't do in front of you and Amber. That's why I don't blame you for wanting a divorce. I'm not the same person you married. If I can't live with me, how can I expect you to?

I'm looking at my rifle right now and wondering for the millionth time what hot brass tastes like. Racking a round in the chamber, sticking the muzzle in your mouth and . . . I don't have to say the rest. Not an hour goes by that I don't wonder. Theres only one thing I know for sure. Whatever happens, it's going to be a relief.

By the time you get this letter, I'll have done what I need to do. You and Amber will get my death benefit. Its way more than I'll ever be worth to you.

Someday when shes old enough to understand, please tell her that I loved her. And that I tried my best.

I know when you read this you'll be sad. But try to remember that I won't be in pain anymore. It'll be better this way.

Love,
Brad

DAD

How're you feeling, son?"

I'm sitting on the back deck, gazing up at the moonless night sky. The Milky Way is a hazy diagonal across the star-glittery blackness. In the immensely vast universe, we are a tiniest speck. In the billions of years of history, we are the merest infinitesimal instant.

Yet we persist in believing that what we do can be important.

"Jake?"

"Sorry, Dad, I was just thinking."

He pulls a chair beside mine and sits. Ice clinks in two glasses. He hands one to me. "You ready?"

He's talking about getting on the plane to Washington and Walter Reed Hospital tomorrow morning.

"I guess."

"You guess?"

Does he want to hear something more affirmative? More

gung-ho? Something like "Can't wait to get my cast off and go back over there and kill me some more insurgents."

He is the father and I am the son. And yet, he is the one who has never had to take another human's life in the line of duty. He's the innocent, who doesn't have to go through life with the guilt, shame, and agony of knowing what you've done and can never undo. I am the one with blood on my hands.

And like Brad knew all too well, it never washes off.

The glass Dad's given me is cold and wet. I take a sip and feel the hot trail of bourbon down my throat. A week ago I came home knowing what the bare minimum was. I had to see Morpiss. I had to tell Erin Rose that she had nothing to be ashamed of or feel guilty about. But I also came home hoping I might be able to do more. That perhaps I could tell the truth as I've come to see it.

There is no glory in war.

There is no honor in killing.

No matter where they send you to fight, innocent people will die.

Military recruiters can't tell the truth because if they did, only the insane would enlist.

Everyone who enters battle comes back wounded. But those wounds aren't always to the flesh, and aren't always visible.

If they could do it all over again, a lot of the guys I served with wouldn't.

A week ago I came home to do more than the bare

minimum, but I failed. Because I may be a hero, but I'm still afraid of bringing shame and embarrassment to my family.

Because for all the things that are wrong with the military, we still need and depend on it to protect us.

Because so many good people have died or been maimed, and so many families have suffered the loss of loved ones. Just so that we Americans can enjoy the freedoms we have.

And finally, because I honestly believe that if there was a better, more humane way than war to protect our country, the United States Armed Forces would be the first to use it.

In the dark beside me, I hear the ice clink in Dad's glass as he takes a sip. "I've been dreading this moment, Jake," he says. "You may think I don't know what you've been going through, but I think I do."

That could mean a lot of things. I glance at him uncertainly. He's hunched forward in his chair, cupping his drink with both hands.

He sits back and sighs. "Son, if I could do it over again." Then he shakes his head. "No, it wouldn't be any different."

"What, Dad?"

"Sometimes I think the only reason I entered the service was because of Uncle David."

I'm confused. Uncle David was the Vietnam draft dodger. The one who brought shame upon the Liddells. But what could that have to do with Dad entering the military? He's not making a whole lot of sense.

"I would have signed up anyway," Dad continues, his shoulders stooped. "I never had the guts Uncle David had."

"Guts to be a draft dodger?" I ask skeptically. This is *really* starting to make no sense.

"In the Liddell family? You better believe it. Going into the service was the *easy* way. David could have taken the route I took. He could have had a desk job far from the action."

But that's not what Dad's always said kept him from active duty. "I thought it was your knee."

He takes another sip. It has to be my imagination, but it feels like the air changes around us.

"Knees are tricky, Jake. The Army docs gave me the benefit of the doubt. But . . ." Dad hesitates. If he's going to say what I think he's going to say, this can't be easy. "The truth is, I could have seen active duty. . . if I'd wanted."

He knows this isn't what he's led me to believe. He always made it sound like he'd been ready to do battle, but the Army doctors said no. "Dad, you're . . . you're saying you didn't want to be in the Army?"

We may only be the tiniest speck of dirt and time in the universe, but this moment is HUGE for me . . . and for him. "I had no choice, Jake," Dad says. "It was bad enough to have one turncoat among us. The Liddells have been a military family for almost as long as the General's has. Could you imagine us having two deserters? We would have been the laughingstock of the military."

I'm still perplexed. "So you're saying *you* think Uncle David was right to be a draft dodger?"

Somewhere out in the dark, a dog starts to bark, and then a second joins in. Blue, who's been sleeping on the terrace beside us, raises his head as if trying to decide whether it's worth the energy to join in. His head goes back down. Guess it wasn't.

Dad takes another sip. "It was Vietnam. Not the Second World War, which was clearly a war of good versus evil. It wasn't like the wars we're fighting today, which, I guess you'd say are wars of sanity versus insanity. Vietnam was different. A difficult war to get behind. All those men dying in a tiny country eight thousand miles away. Meanwhile, our country was never in any danger of attack. There was no threat of terrorism. Nothing like 9/11 or any of these other terrible bombings and rampage shootings. In Vietnam, all we were fighting against was some vague idea called the domino theory. An unproven fear that if South Vietnam fell to the Communists, the rest of Southeast Asia would follow. And then, supposedly, the entire rest of the world."

Despite the long explanation, Dad still hasn't answered my question, which is so big and portentous, that I feel like I have to repeat it. "So . . . you're saying that Uncle David *was right* to dodge the draft?"

Dad's quiet for a bit. Then he says, "Well, let's put it this way. I can't say he was wrong. Not in that particular war. He refused to serve because he sincerely believed that war was immoral. In our family, in this country at that time, that took courage, Jake."

This is stunning. I've been brought up to believe that dodging service in *any* war is the worst sin imaginable. I always knew Dad wasn't the most gung-ho soldier. But I figured that was because, with his bad knee, he was resigned to being a career desk jockey. It never occurred to me that he might have *wanted* it that way.

In the dark, Dad turns to me. Without the moonlight, his face is just a shadow. "I want you to know something, Jake. As far as I am concerned, you don't have to get on that plane tomorrow morning. You can stay here. Do your physical therapy here, and consider your service to the military complete. If that's what you decide to do, I will stand behind you and support you in every way I can."

"If I don't get on that plane, I'll be AWOL."

Dad bends forward, takes another sip of bourbon, and shakes his head slowly. "No, son. The General won't allow that to happen. You're the one thing he's always wanted, another hero to carry on the family tradition. Believe me, if you don't want to go back, he'll find a way to make sure you get your medal *and* an honorable discharge. He'll do whatever he has to do to avoid that embarrassment. And he has connections to do it."

I'm speechless. In a week filled with the unexpected, this is the surprise that truly rocks my world. I really *don't* have to go back. My father doesn't want me to, and the General can't stop me.

But wait, isn't this exactly the kind of nepotistic advantage I never wanted? I was so dead set on proving I could do it on my own.

"You'll be alive," Dad says as if he knows what I'm thinking. "You've proven yourself, son. You've risked your life to save other men. You've been wounded in battle. You've done far more than you had to. But if you go back over there and something bad happens . . ."

In the distance, tires screech as some road warrior jumps a green light. A dog starts to bark again. I sit back, stare at the night sky, feel my insides swirl. He's left something unspoken. Six years ago we lost Mom. If anything happens to me, half his family will be gone. Dad's not just telling me I don't have to go back. He's practically begging me not to.

BRAD

I was in the barracks, sitting on my bed with my laptop. It was the tail end of a two-day sandstorm. Even inside the barracks, sand got into everything. In our armpits and pubic hair. In our noses and mouths.

I was playing *Minecraft*, the perfect escape. Morpiss had shown us the trick to playing in storms—cover the laptop with cling wrap. I just needed two more Eye of Enders and I'd be at the End.

The barracks door banged open and Magnet stuck his head in. "It's Sergeant Burrows!"

In a flash I was on my feet, running out into the impossibly bright, hot, dusty sunlight.

"Locked himself in the crapper!" Magnet yelled over his shoulder as I followed him.

I heard the screaming long before I got there. It sounded like someone in horrible pain. Like Morpiss after the land mine. Like half the dozen other guys I'd heard scream in searing unbearable pain. A scream so agonizing that you knew that whatever had happened, the guy was never going to be the same.

A small crowd of soldiers had collected around the crapper, a twenty-foot Conex with a steel door. You'd need an acetylene torch or a cutoff tool to get in. The PFCs, corporals, even another sergeant, all parted when I arrived. Like I was a colonel or something. Of course, it was only because they knew I was the closest thing Brad had to a battle buddy.

The screams continued. It sounded like Brad was being tortured. Which, in a way, he was. I pressed my cheek against the warm steel door. His cries were so harsh you could feel the metal vibrate.

"Sergeant Burrows," I said when he paused to take a breath.

Another scream followed, but it was shorter.

"Sarge," I said at the next pause.

"Morpiss!" Brad wailed and then started to sob.

"Not your fault, Sarge." I sensed it was too soon to ask him to let me in. I had to talk him down first.

He roared with agony. A lion with his foot in a trap.

"Sarge, we've been over this before," I said patiently and calmly. "You followed protocol. Did what you were supposed to do."

"Those kids!" he cried.

"They were attacking us, Sarge. They would have killed us if they could. It was us or them."

"*Ahhhh!*" he screamed again. He was in agony. Even if he'd done nothing wrong, men had been horribly maimed on his watch. That mother with the burned infant. The time in a dark basement when he'd found a half-dead, delirious torture victim whose ankles had been bored through with an electric drill. Brad was drowning in waking nightmares. Trying to be logical with him wouldn't work because there was nothing logical about the way he was thinking. No human brain that's marinated in a lethal mixture of guilt and trauma and half a dozen different medications can be expected to be logical.

"You've got Amber, Sarge," I reminded him, even though I wasn't sure it would help. Erin Rose had told him she wanted a divorce. It was hard to imagine how his daughter would ever be a significant presence in his life.

"I can't. I can't," he gasped. "It's . . . killing me."

I didn't have to ask if he had a weapon. Of course he did. Any soldier who locks himself in the crapper and starts screaming like a madman knows what's going to happen if he comes out alive.

His career was over. Now it was a matter of life or death. "People love you, Sarge. They respect you. You're a good man and a good soldier who volunteered to do things no one else wanted to do. I know what you're feeling right now is horrible. But it won't last. You know how it is. It comes and goes. It passes."

There was silence. I looked up at the concerned, aching faces of the soldiers around me. Brad had been a brave soldier. He'd seen action. He'd stood his ground. He'd protected his men.

The silence from inside worried me. It meant he was thinking. And right now, whatever he was thinking couldn't be good. "Sarge, you hear what I just said? It feels really bad now, but it'll pass."

"But . . . it always comes back."

For a moment I was stymied. I knelt beside the crapper door, in the heat and dust, asking myself, *How do you respond to that?* How do you convince someone who's been in terrible pain for months that it's magically going to go away?

I never got the chance to come up with an answer.

When the gunshot came, a couple of guys jumped. I felt like the bullet had gone through me, too. Someone ran to get a cutting tool. I sat in the hot, dusty sunlight and sobbed.

Like a lot of good soldiers, Staff Sergeant Bradley Burrows had taken on jobs that no one else had wanted. And like a lot of soldiers, what he'd agreed to do had broken him. Just as it would have broken any normal human being.

ONE YEAR LATER

Wearing fatigues and body armor, carrying packs and small arms, a group of us are humping across an open field. *Snap!* A single shot and one of our guys goes down. The rest of us immediately hit the dirt.

"Doc!" the wounded soldier shouts.

Two men provide suppressive fire while another soldier and I crawl to the wounded man and assess his wound. It's not seriously life-threatening, so we drag him to a protected spot and start to administer first aid.

Tweeeeeeeet! A whistle blows. The "wounded" man sits up and brushes himself off. From across the field, a grizzled drill sergeant approaches. "All right, cadets, that's it for field training. Get to class."

When I pull on my rucksack, a textbook falls out. Rucksack weight for these exercises is supposed to be forty-five pounds, but I've been sticking in additional load. It can't hurt to get comfortable with an extra fifteen or twenty pounds.

The drill sergeant reminds me of Sgt. Washington, my old JROTC instructor, only grayer and with deeper lines in his face. But with the same erect military bearing. Same by-the-book attitude. I've just picked up the textbook when he snags it out of my hand and reads the title: "*The Inside Battle: Our Military Mental Health Crisis.*"

His wrinkled eyes narrow. "Mental health, huh? So, cadet, you gonna specialize in EBH?"

"Drill Sergeant, yes I am." Embedded Behavioral Health personnel are placed with the troops in the field. Their job is to identify and respond to emotional problems early and onsite instead of waiting in distant hospitals for soldiers to be brought in after they've crashed and burned. Or, in the case of Brad, soldiers who'll never make it in at all.

The drill sergeant is still holding my textbook. "In Desert Storm, we didn't have any of this mental health stuff."

He not only looks like an old-timer, he sounds like one. So I answer with: "With all due respect for your many years of service, Sergeant, the rate of suicide among veterans of Desert Storm is unacceptably high. We have to do a better job of taking care of the soldiers who risk their lives to protect us. Honestly, it's the very least we can do."

The drill sergeant glances at my name tag, then opens the textbook to the front page, where I've written my full name and barracks back at Fort Sam.

"Jake Liddell," he says. Some people around here

look surprised when they find out who I am. But not him. "Silver Star, right?"

"Affirmative, Sergeant."

He hands the book back. "Those Desert Storm veterans who've committed suicide? Some were my buddies. It's a tragedy. A real tragedy." He pats me on the shoulder. "You're doing a good thing, Cadet Liddell. Now get to class."

I speak to Aurora nearly every day, but only get to see her a couple of times a week. She's moved here to San Antonio, where she's sharing an apartment with another dental hygienist, and working at the Joint Base San Antonio– Randolph Dental Clinic. I have the General to thank for that. He leaned on some of his connections to get her the job. After I decided to transfer to Fort Sam Houston for Army medical training, Aurora and I had a long talk. She insisted that she and Doug were never anything more than "good friends." She also wanted to know about the evening her friend Emily drove past the park and saw me with Brandi in a "compromised position." That was why Aurora wasn't answering my calls or texts the day before I left for Walter Reed. She said she'd needed time to think.

She accepted my explanation and knows that Brandi and I are still in touch. It's not something I tell many people, but I support Brandi's campaign for more transparency regarding JROTC's relationship to the armed forces. I also support her argument that a disproportionate number of minorities and financially disadvantaged people are forced to enlist for lack of better opportunities.

Not long ago, a fellow cadet here at Fort Sam told me that what first got him interested in the military was playing *Call of Duty*. I knew how he felt. I've played it too. It's fun and exciting. But don't kid yourself. Don't think for an instant that a video game is anything like real war. No game results in a dick-shrinking terror so bad that you want to cry. So bad that you wished to God you were anywhere but there. So bad that you can't believe this is something you voluntarily signed up for.

Playing video games doesn't result in pain so unbelievably severe that you want to bite your tongue in half just to feel some relief.

There's no heavy metal soundtrack when you're in a real firefight. The terror is real. The pain is real. Death is real.

Our country came into being as the result of a war. And even though former President Ronald Regan once said that people free to choose will always choose peace, America has managed to be involved in some war somewhere for all but 17 of the past 240 years. I don't know why it has to be that way, but I don't have a suggestion for changing it either.

As long as America continues in its Forever War, it will need soldiers. They will always be young, but they need not always have stars in their eyes and misplaced dreams of glory in their hearts. Those who choose to serve should be given an honest assessment of what lies ahead.

Rarely does anyone become a hero without paying a terrible price.

POSTSCRIPT

"I am tired and sick of war . . . It is only those who have neither fired a shot nor heard the shrieks and groans of the wounded who cry aloud for blood, for vengeance, for desolation. War is hell."

—WILLIAM TECUMSEH SHERMAN (1820–1891, UNION GENERAL)